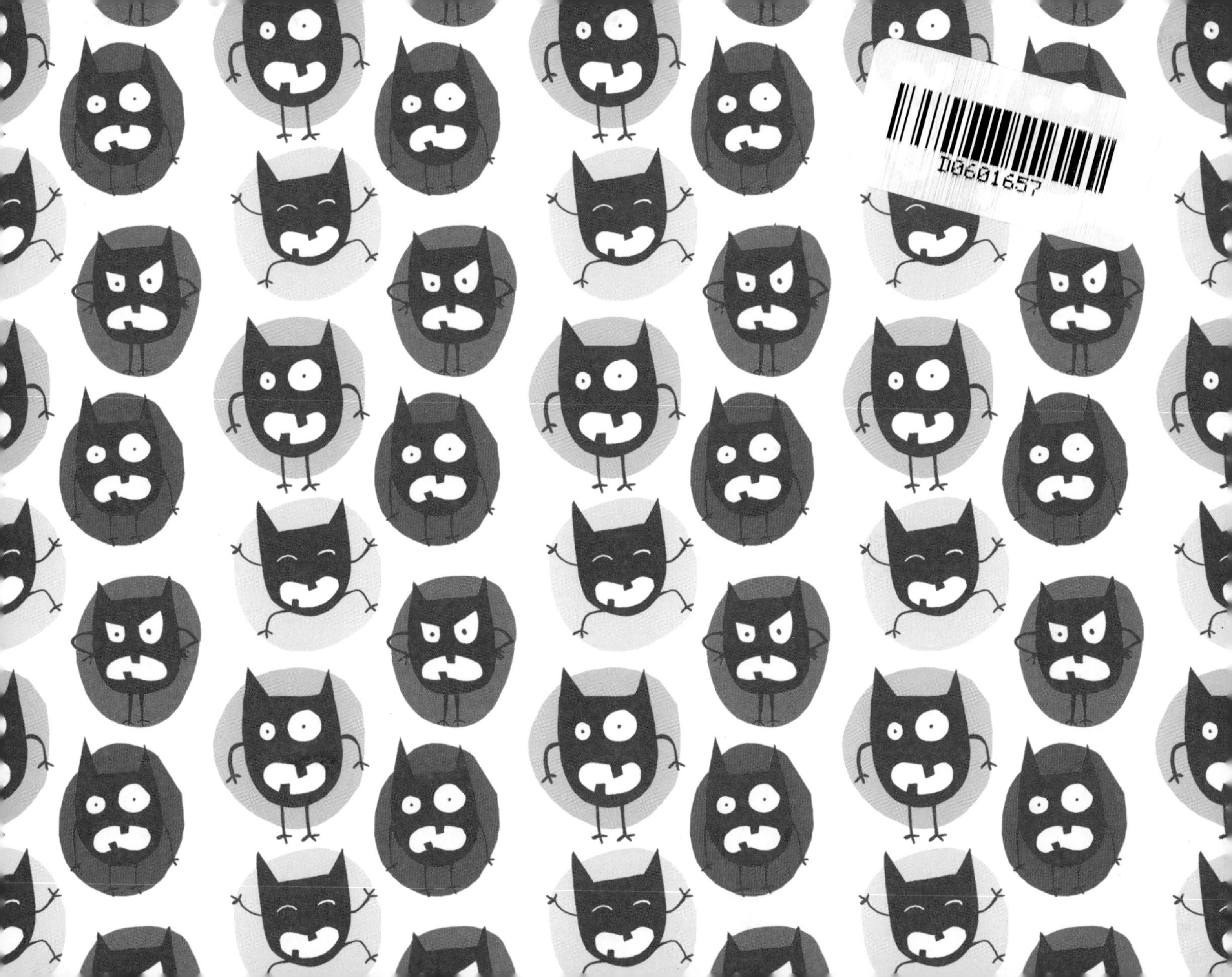

Published in the United States 2010 by
Blue Apple Books
515 Valley Street, Maplewood, NJ 07040
www.blueapplebooks.com

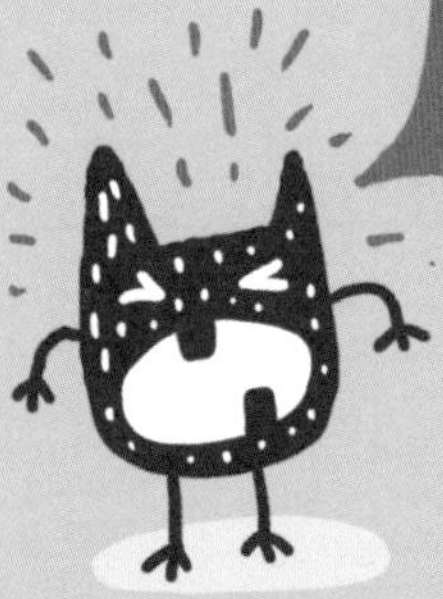

Distributed in the U.S. by Chronicle Books
First Edition
Printed in China 09/10
ISBN: 978-1-60905-037-5

2 4 6 8 10 9 7 5 3 1

Adopt a GLURB!

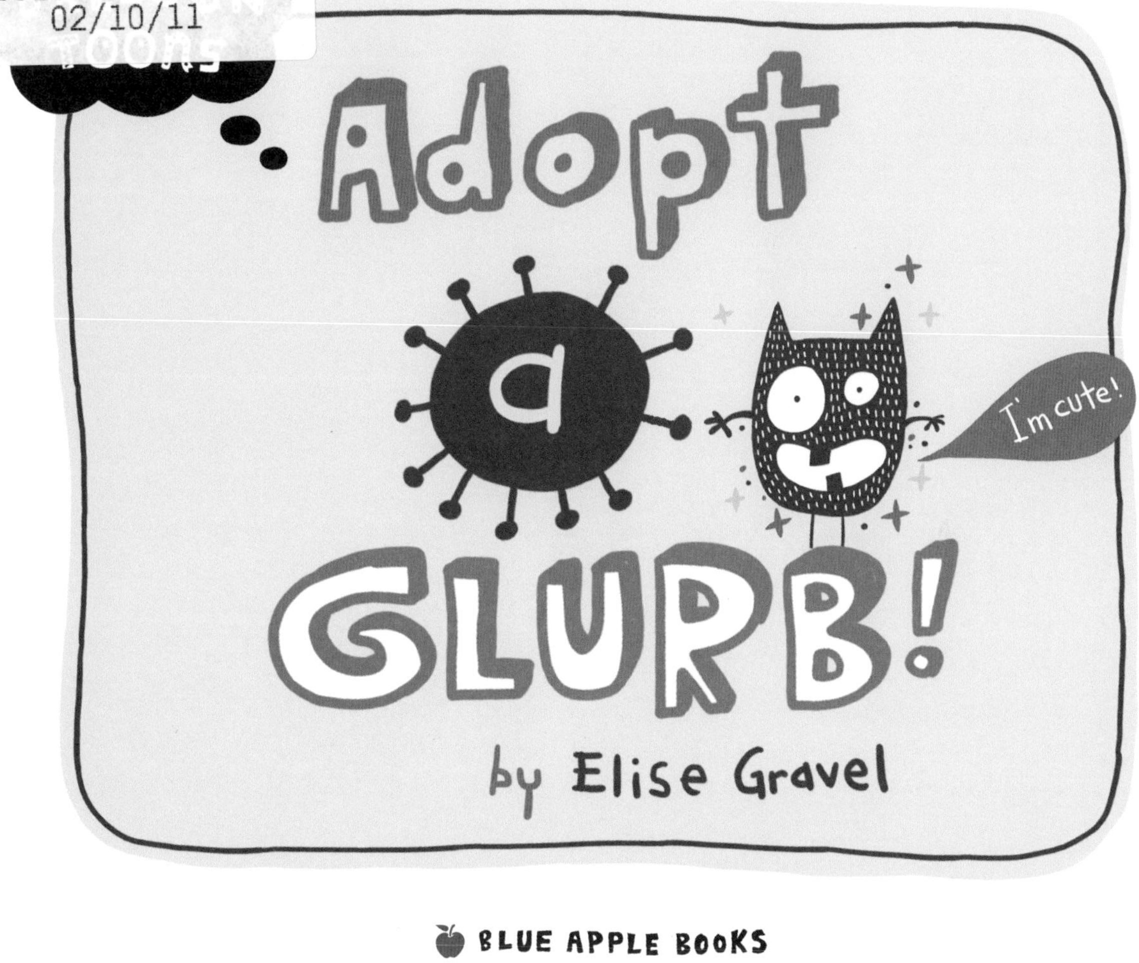
I'm cute!

by Elise Gravel

BLUE APPLE BOOKS

HERE'S THE GLURB

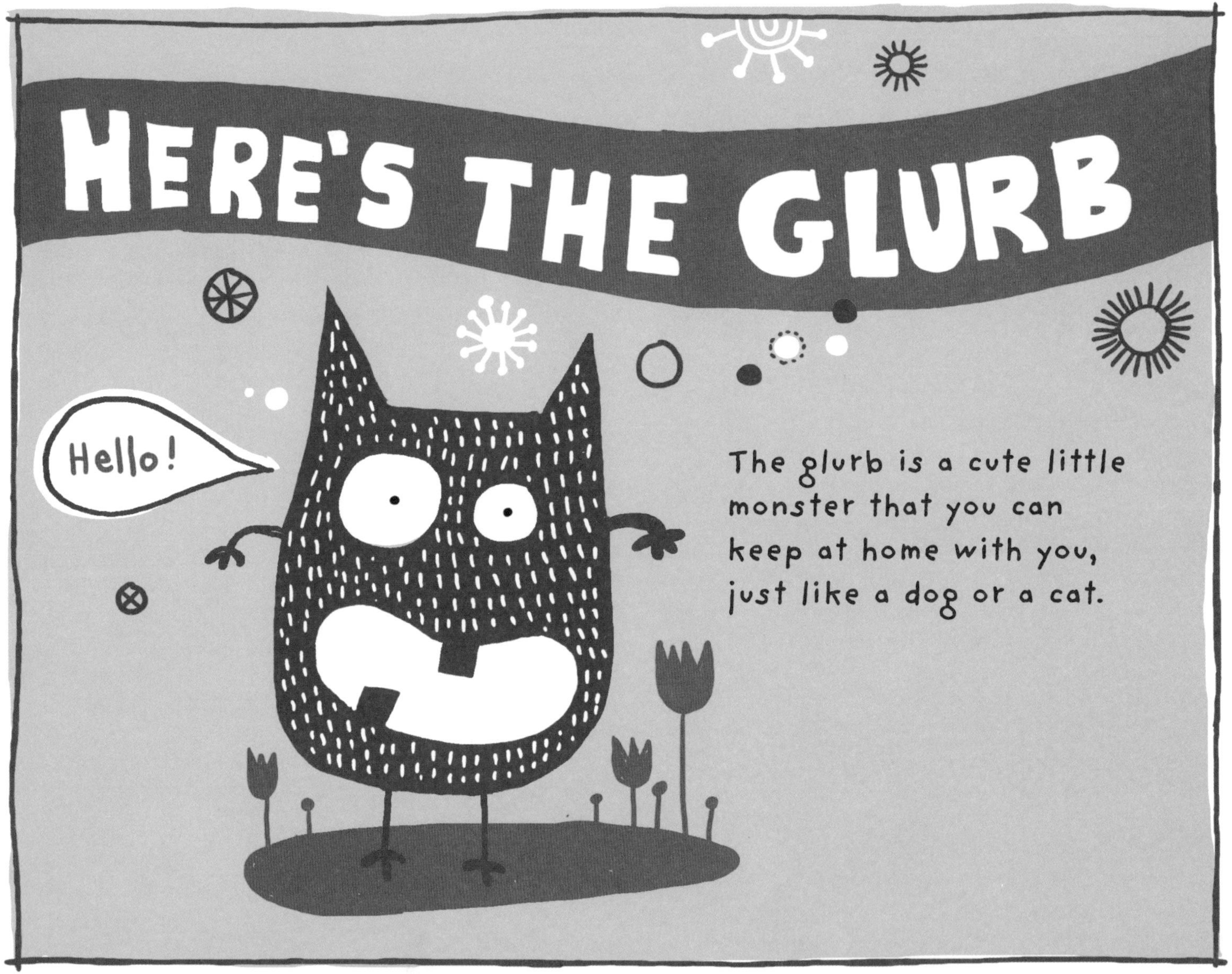
Hello!

The glurb is a cute little monster that you can keep at home with you, just like a dog or a cat.

THE glurb IS VERY FUNNY.

If you don't take good care of him, you'll be in trouble. He's a little RASCAL.

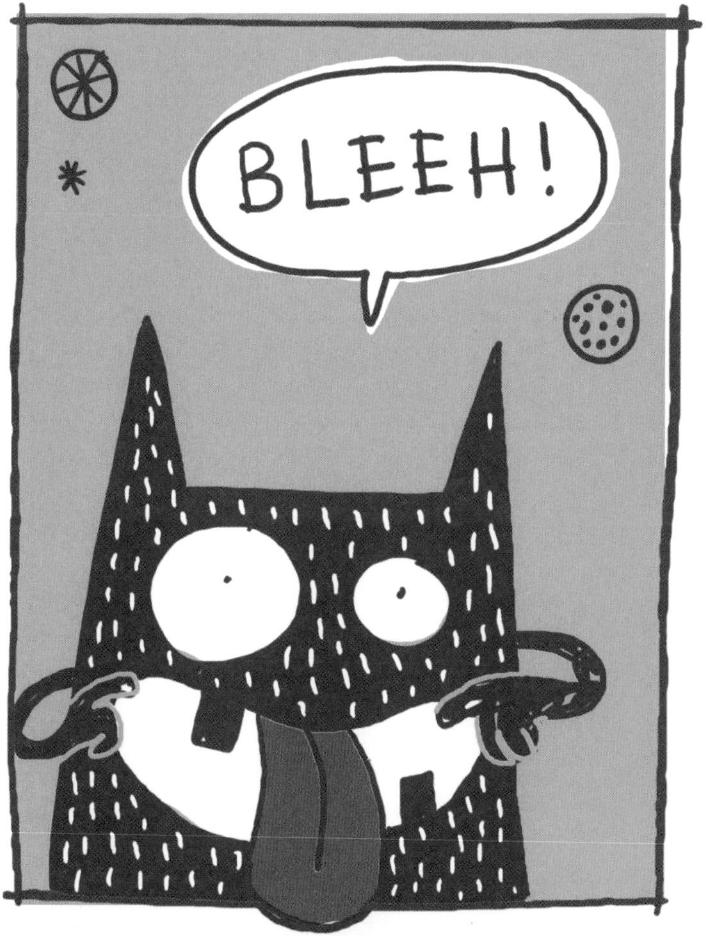
BLEEH!

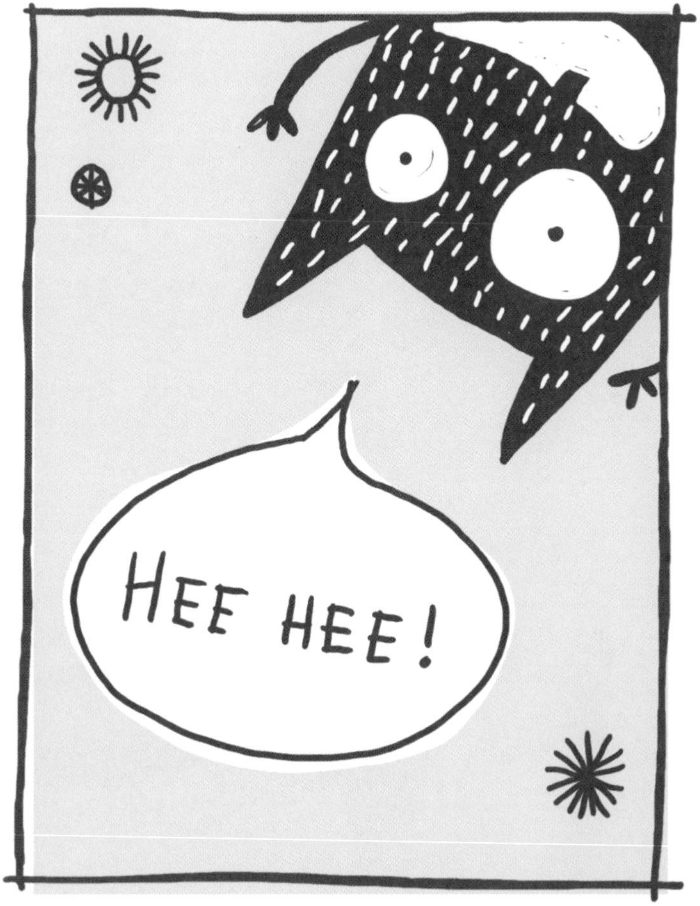
HEE HEE!

Where does the glurb come from?

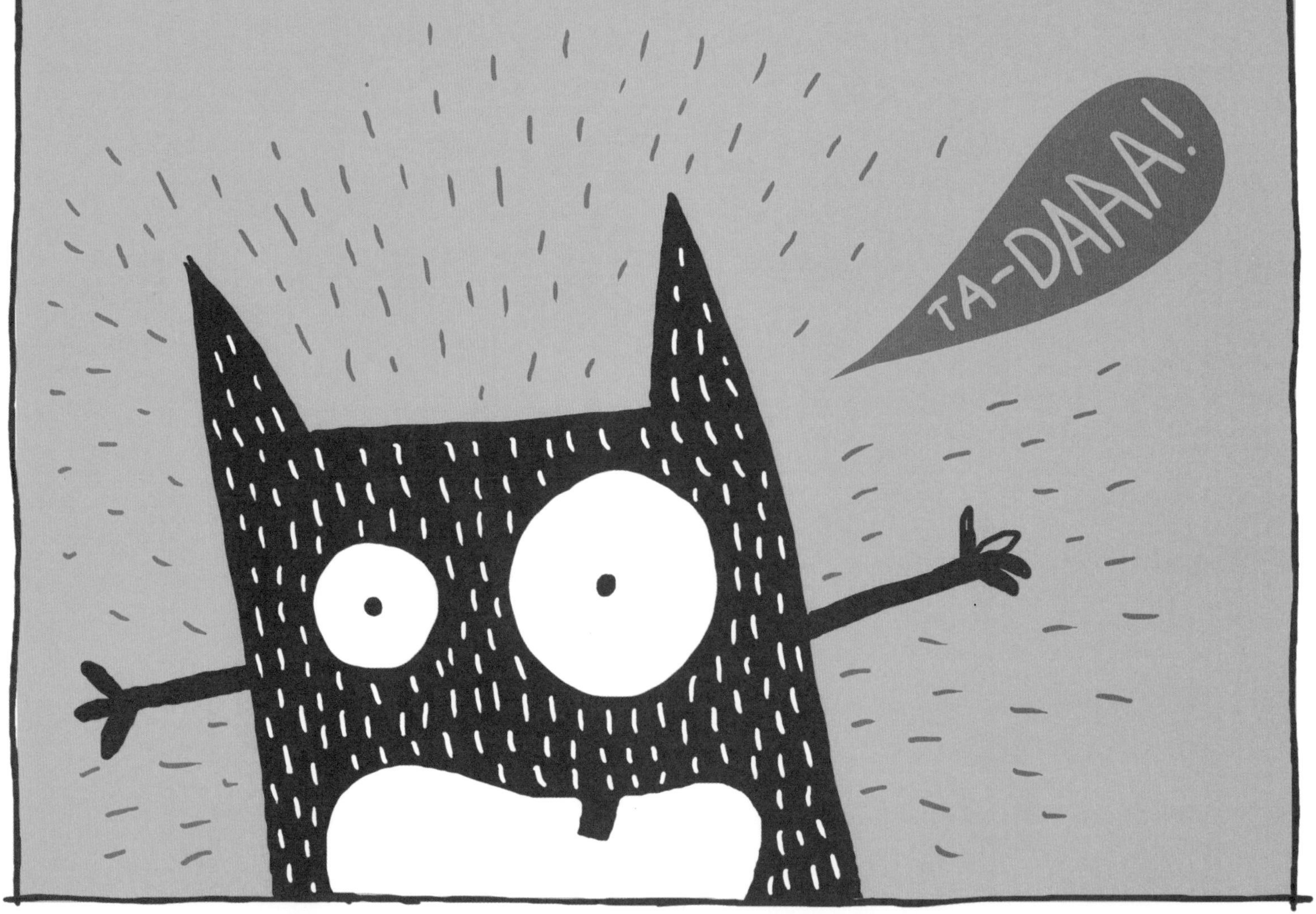
TA-DAAA!

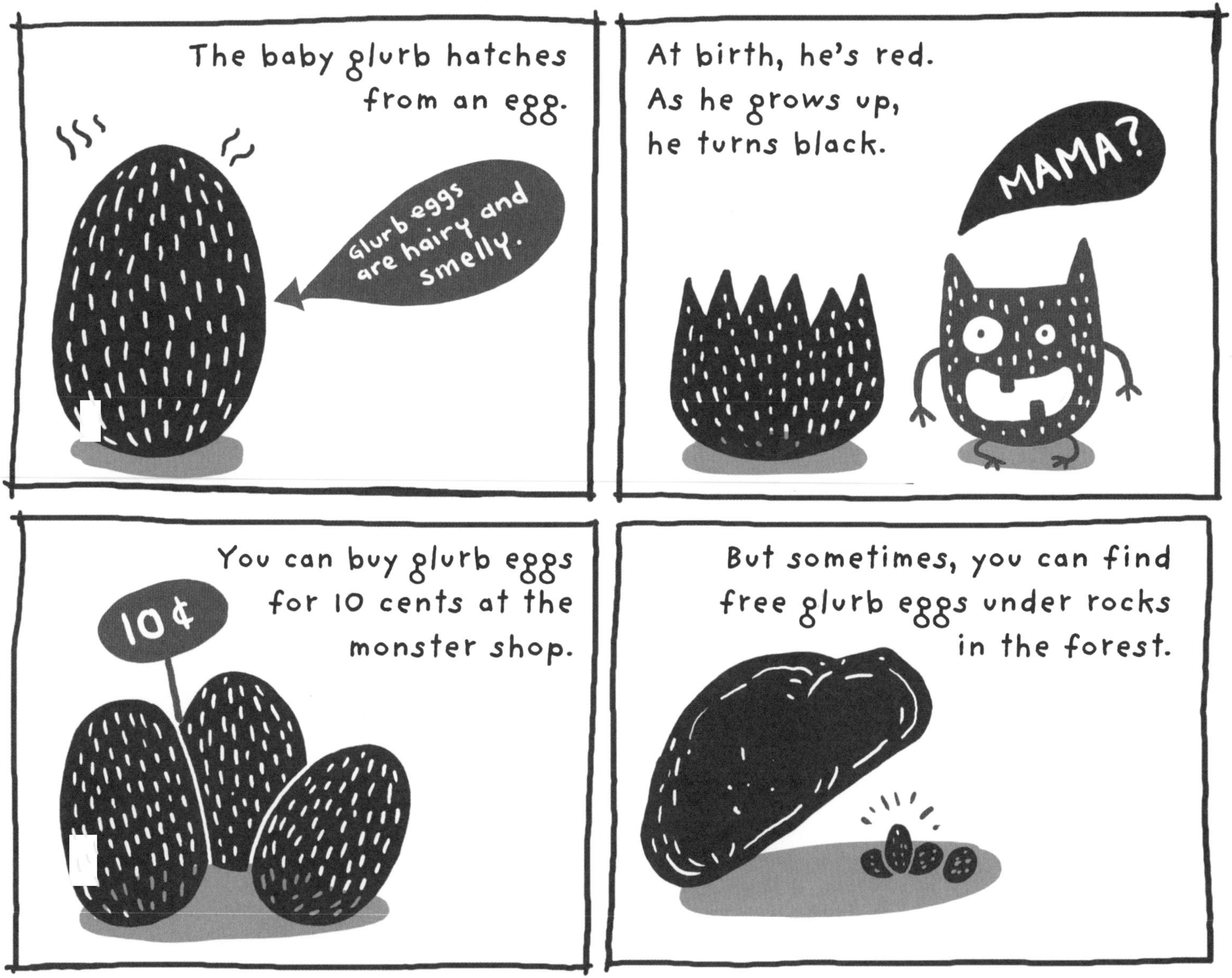
The baby glurb hatches from an egg.
Glurb eggs are hairy and smelly.
At birth, he's red. As he grows up, he turns black.
MAMA?
You can buy glurb eggs for 10 cents at the monster shop.
10¢
But sometimes, you can find free glurb eggs under rocks in the forest.

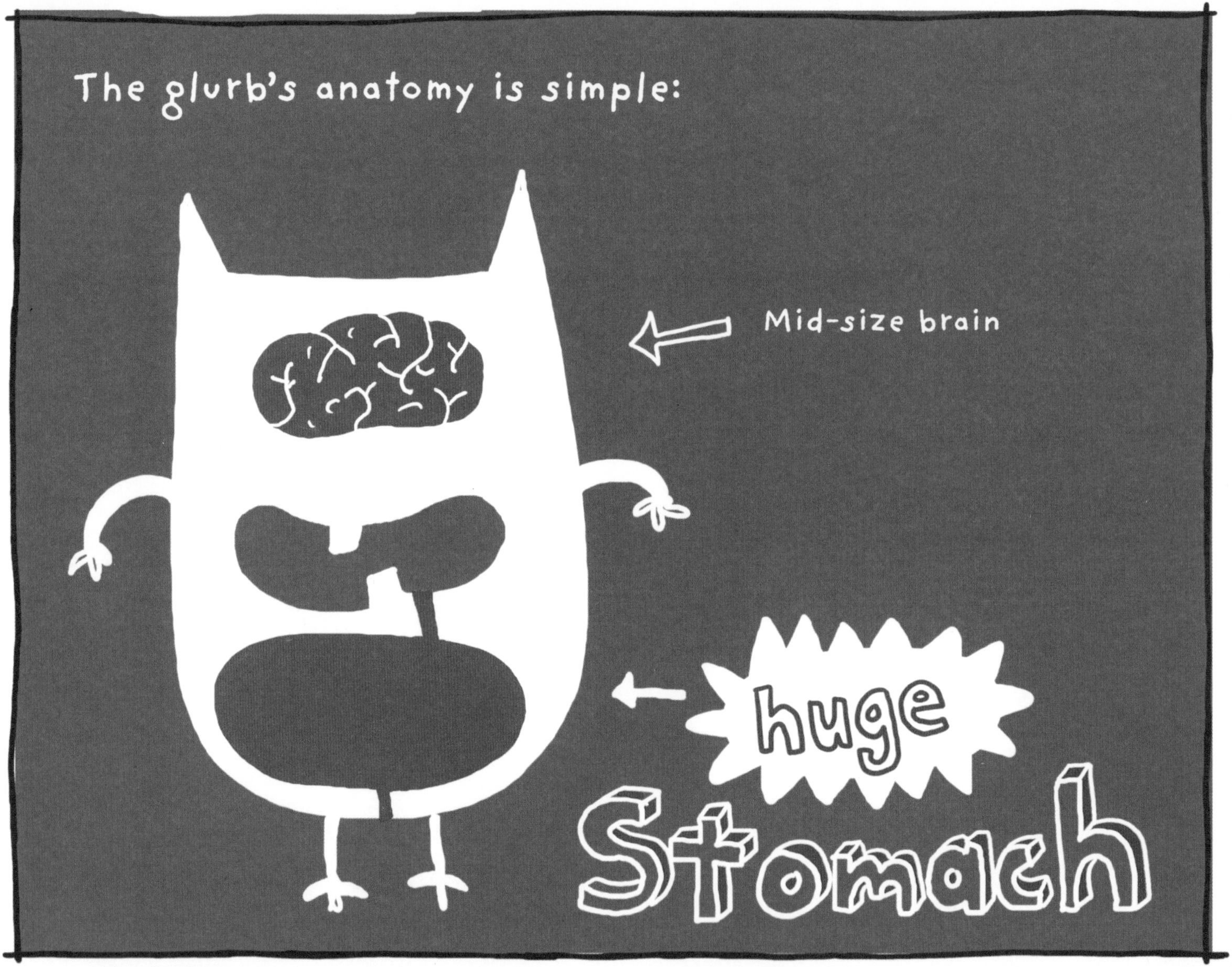

The glurb's anatomy is simple:
Mid-size brain
huge
Stomach

The feet of the glurb stink because they are covered with tiny, sticky, suction cups.

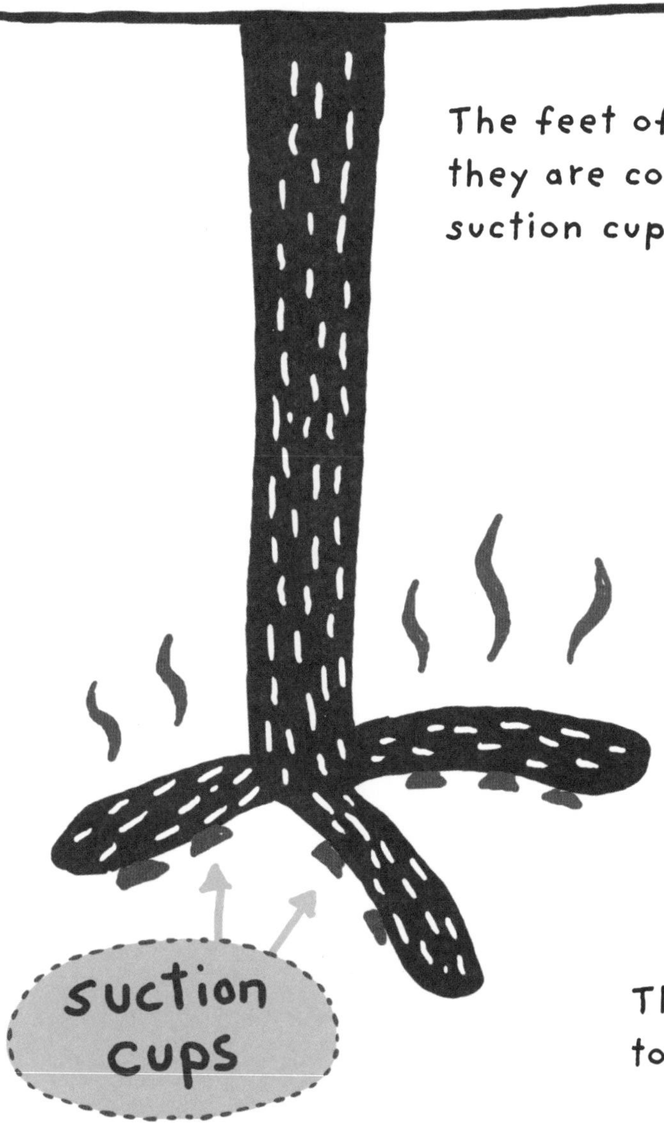
suction cups

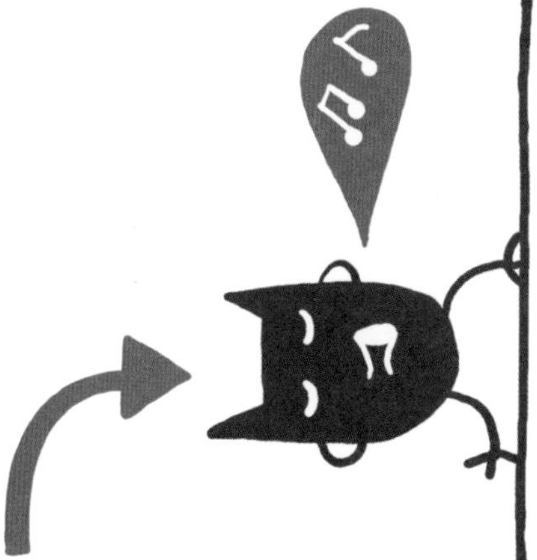

These suction cups allow the glurb to walk on walls or ceilings.

The glurb loves sports.
When you play with him,
please be gentle.
He's a lot smaller
than he thinks.

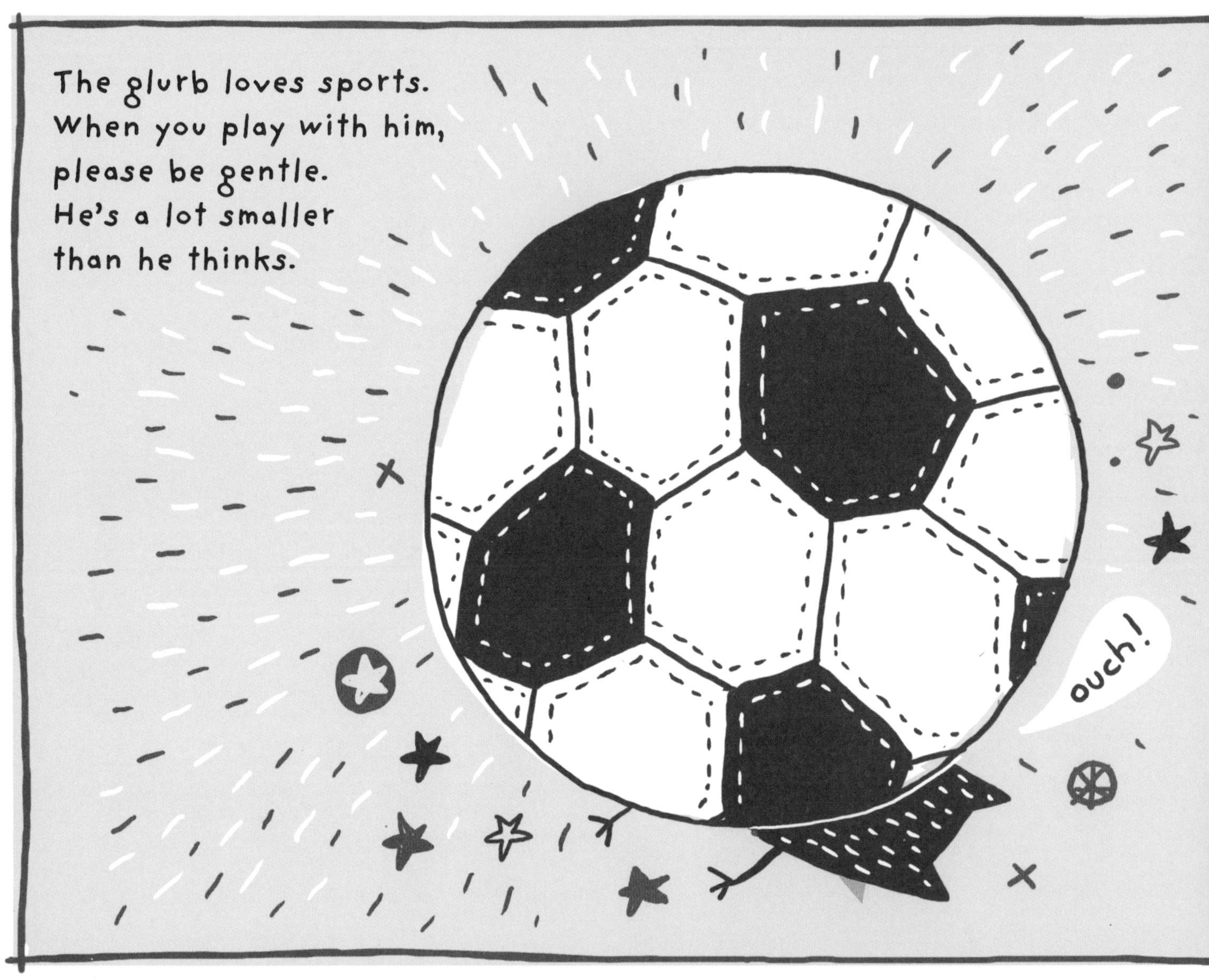
ouch!

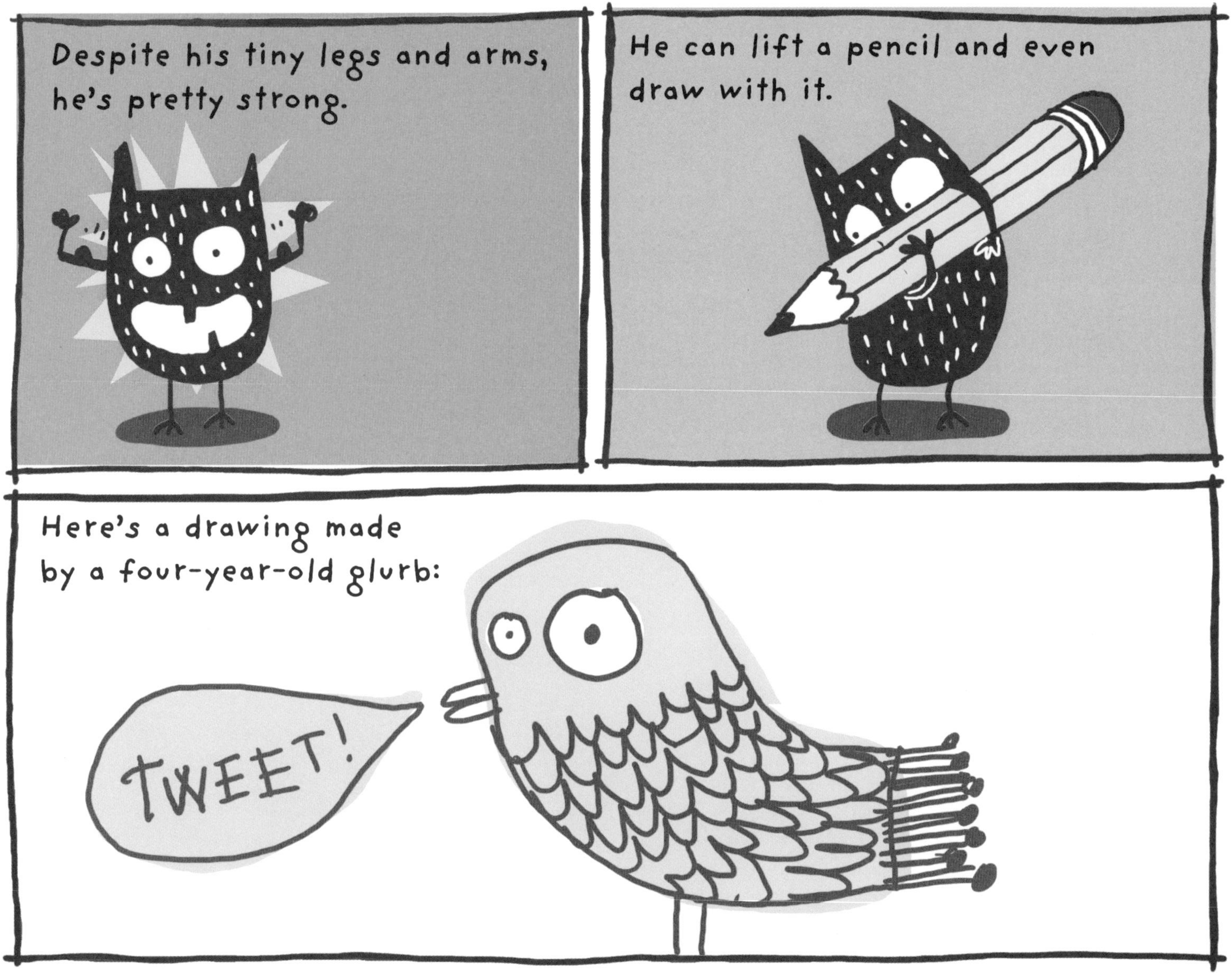
Despite his tiny legs and arms, he's pretty strong.
He can lift a pencil and even draw with it.
Here's a drawing made by a four-year-old glurb:
TWEET!

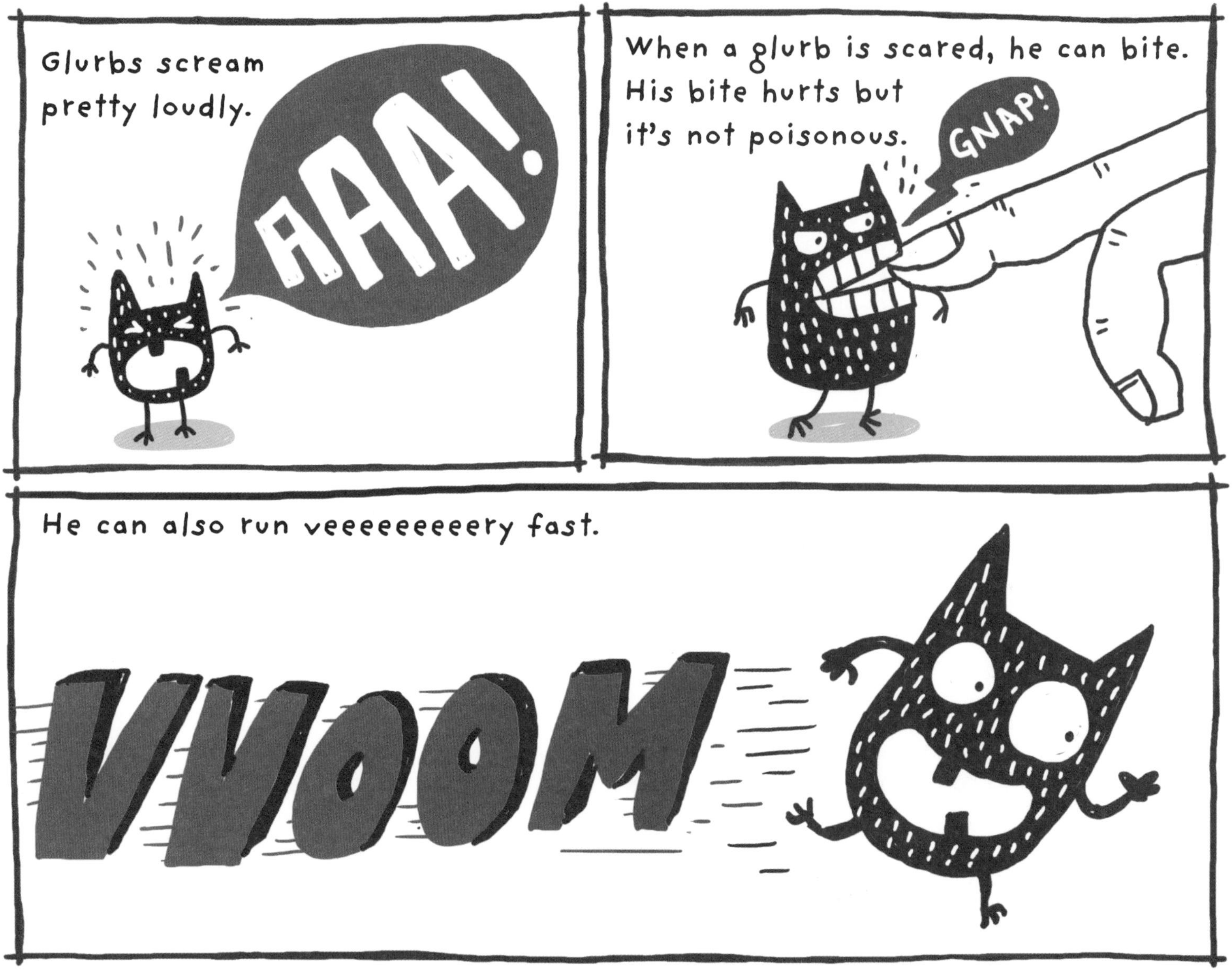
Glurbs scream pretty loudly.
AAA!
When a glurb is scared, he can bite. His bite hurts but it's not poisonous.
GNAP!
He can also run veeeeeeeeery fast.
VVOOM

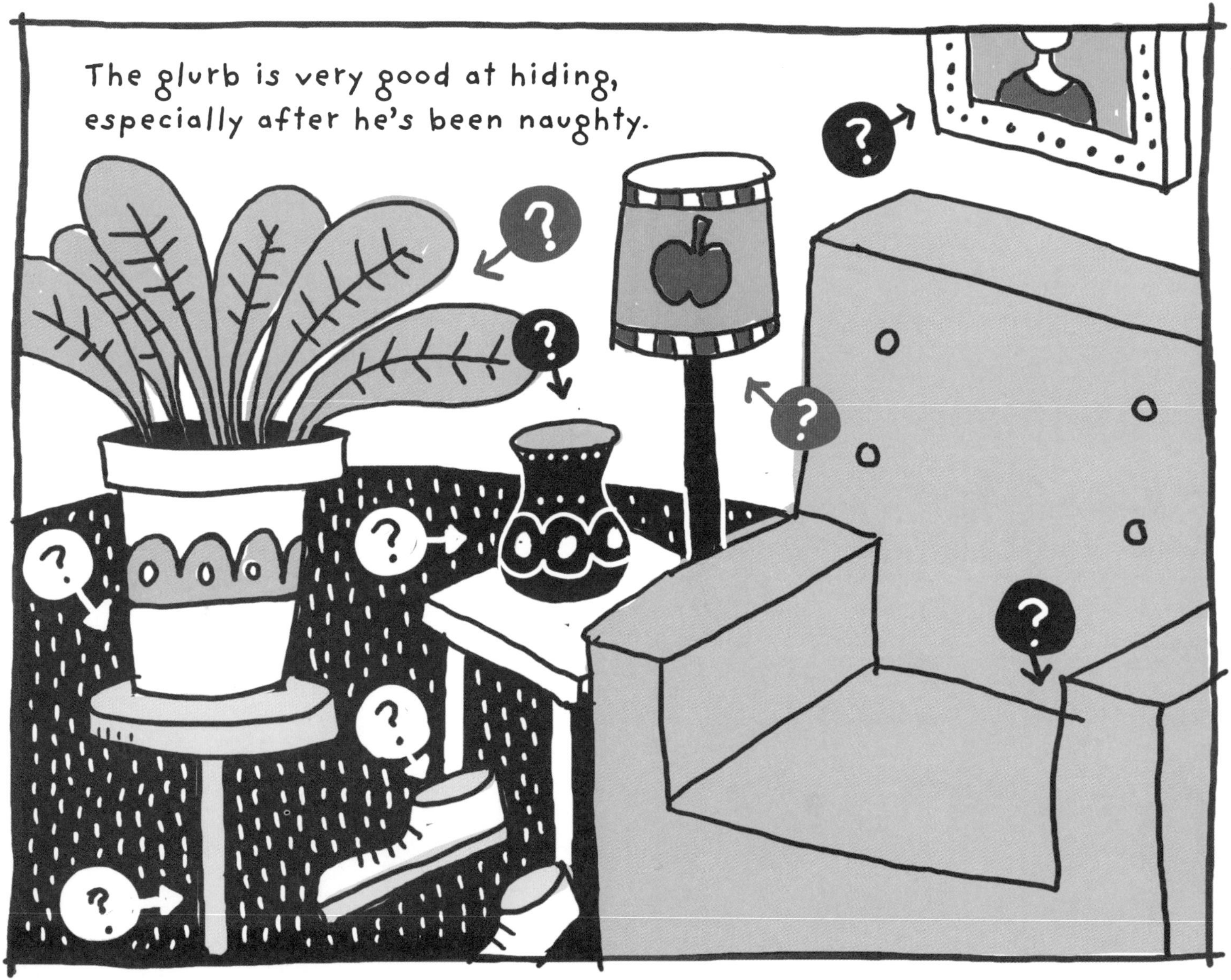
The glurb is very good at hiding,
especially after he's been naughty.

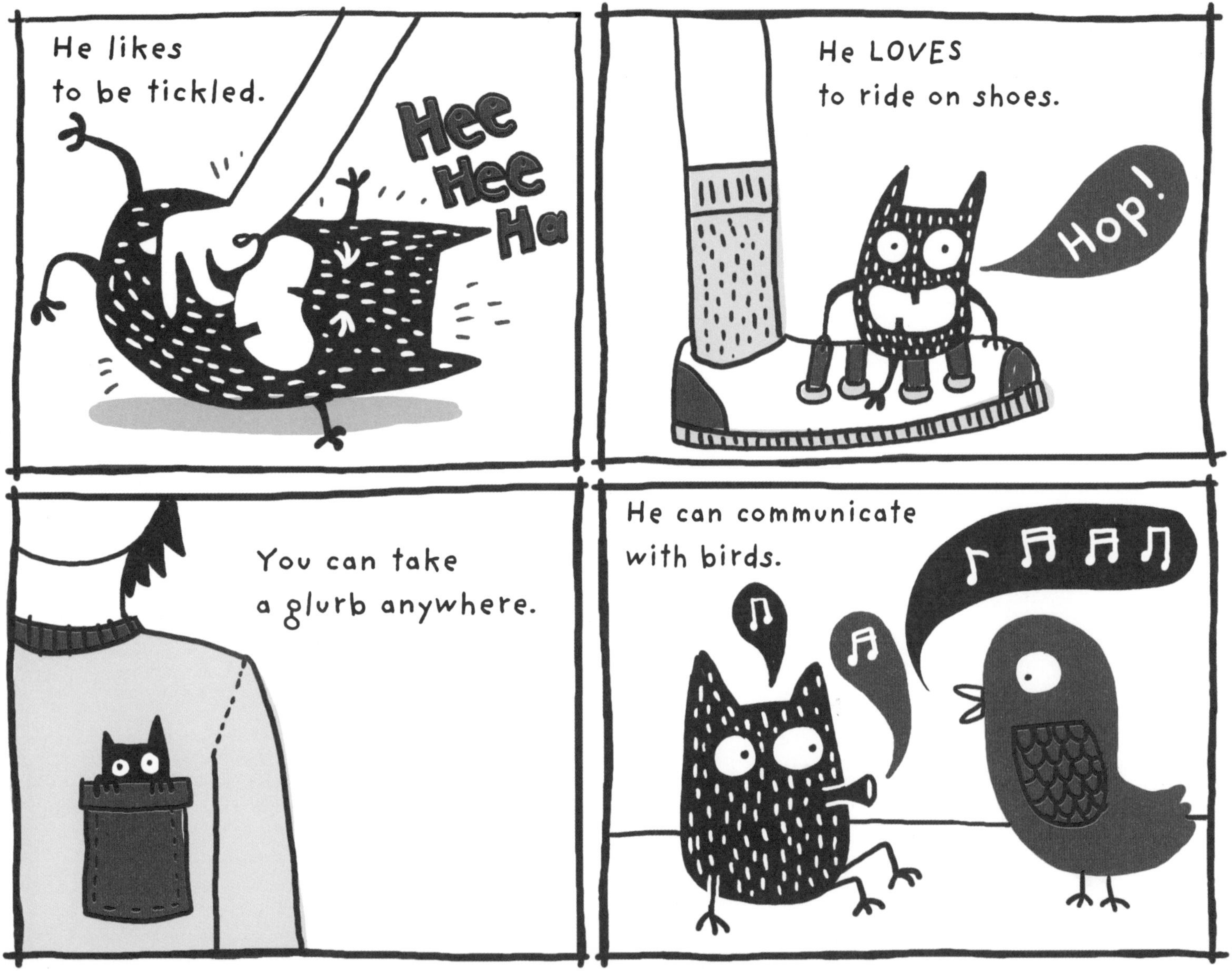
He likes to be tickled.
Hee Hee Ha
He LOVES to ride on shoes.
Hop!
You can take a glurb anywhere.
He can communicate with birds.

His favorite hobby is to unroll toilet paper. If you're a tidy person, maybe the glurb is not a good choice for you.

TAKING CARE OF YOUR GLURB

Be very gentle with your glurb.

Baby glurbs need a lot of love and cuddles. Since a glurb is smelly, it might take you a while to get used to kissing it.

They smell like rotten mustard.

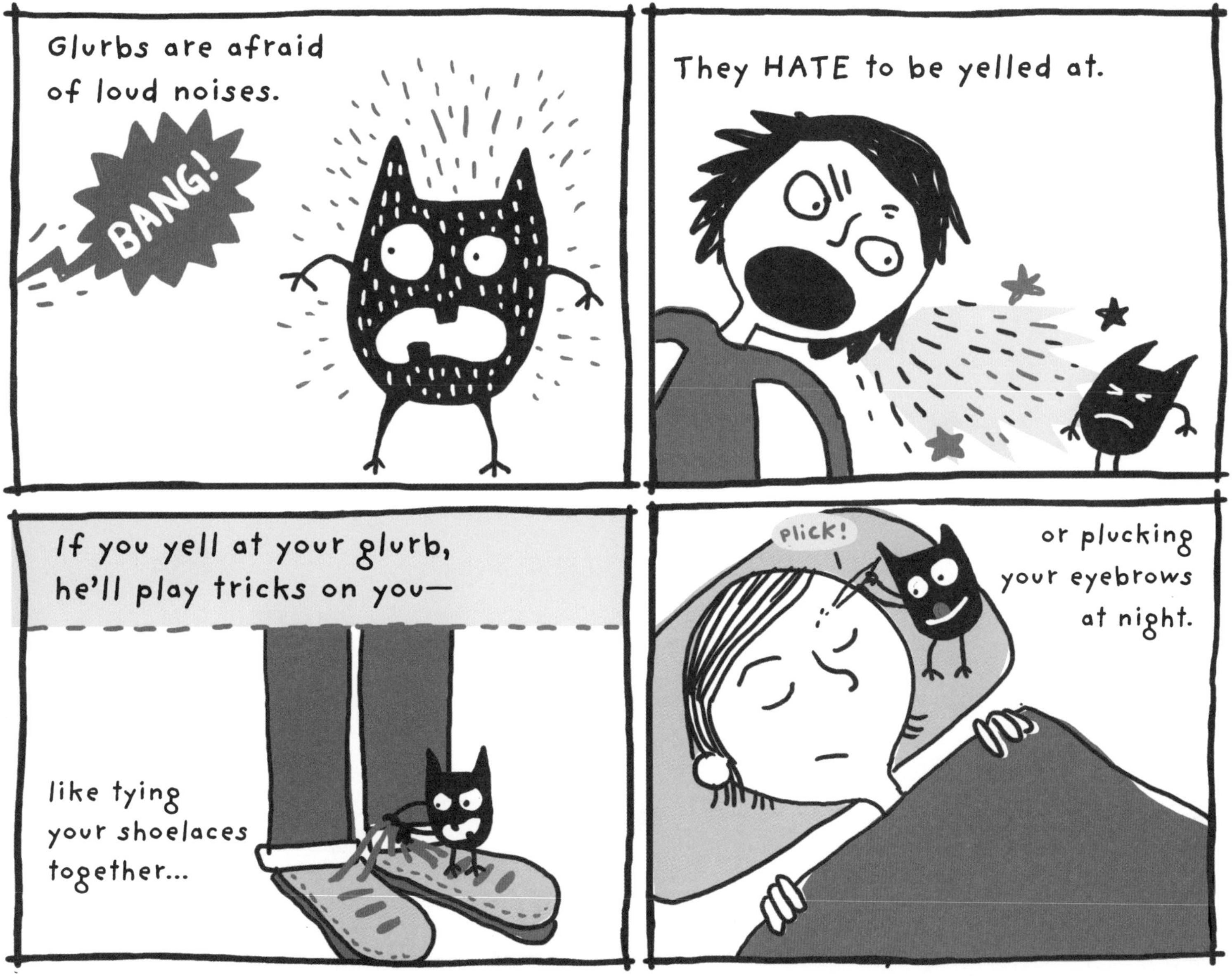
Glurbs are afraid of loud noises.
BANG!
They HATE to be yelled at.
If you yell at your glurb, he'll play tricks on you—
like tying your shoelaces together...
PLICK!
or plucking your eyebrows at night.

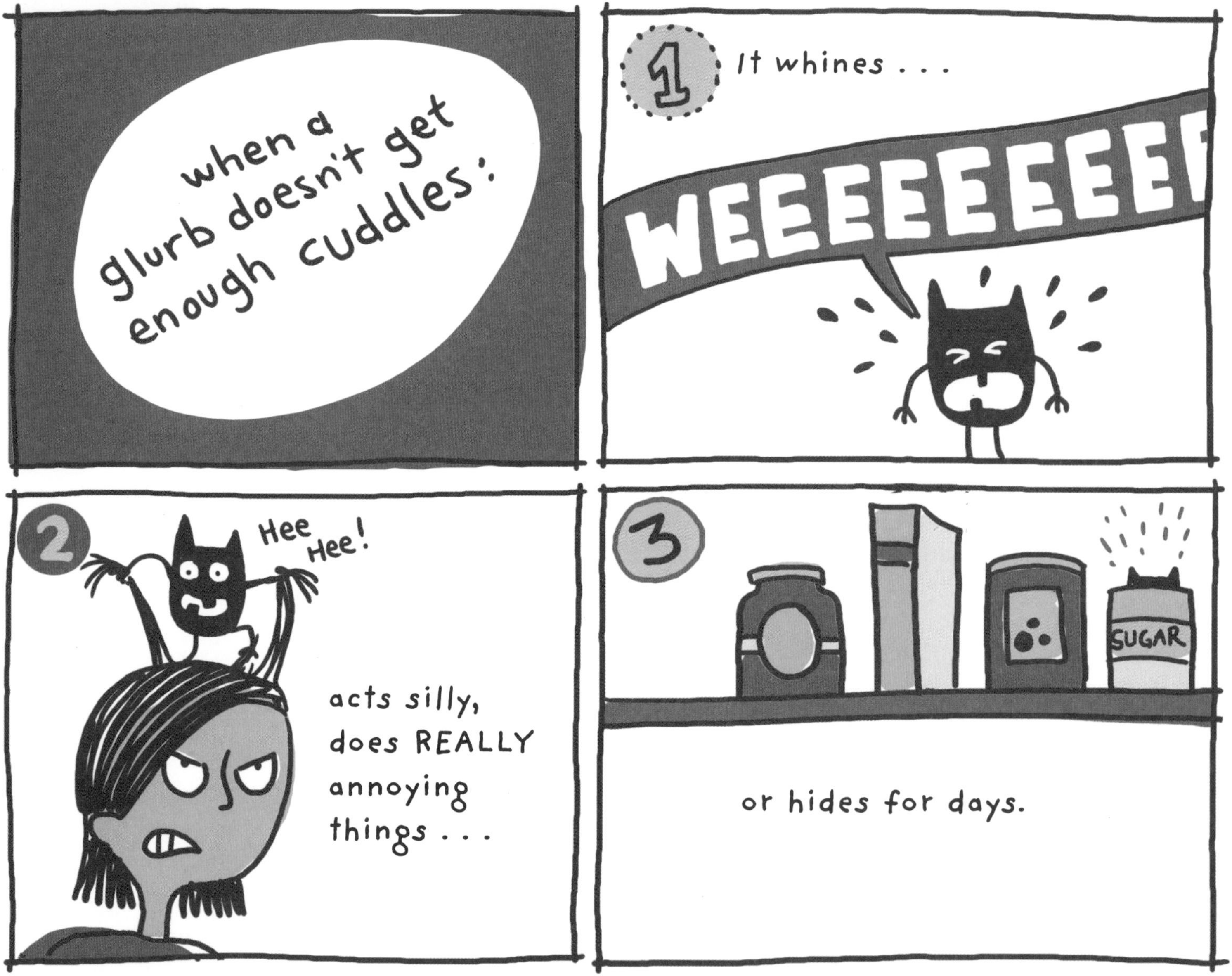
when a glurb doesn't get enough cuddles:
1
It whines . . .
WEEEEEEEEEE
2
Hee Hee!
acts silly, does REALLY annoying things . . .
3
SUGAR
or hides for days.

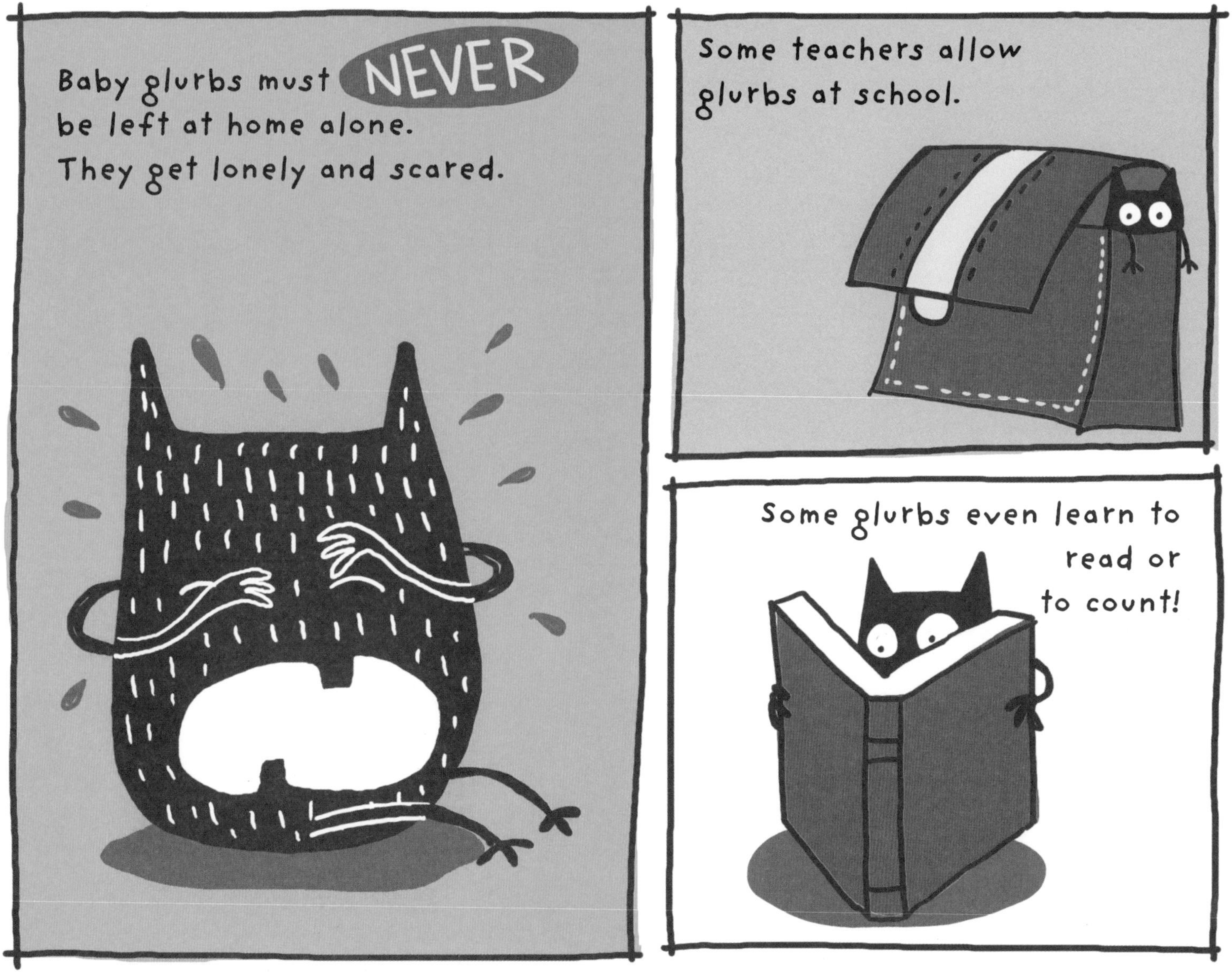
Baby glurbs must NEVER be left at home alone. They get lonely and scared.
Some teachers allow glurbs at school.
Some glurbs even learn to read or to count!

Baby glurbs can have little accidents.

That problem can be easily solved with Glurbies, found wherever diapers are sold.

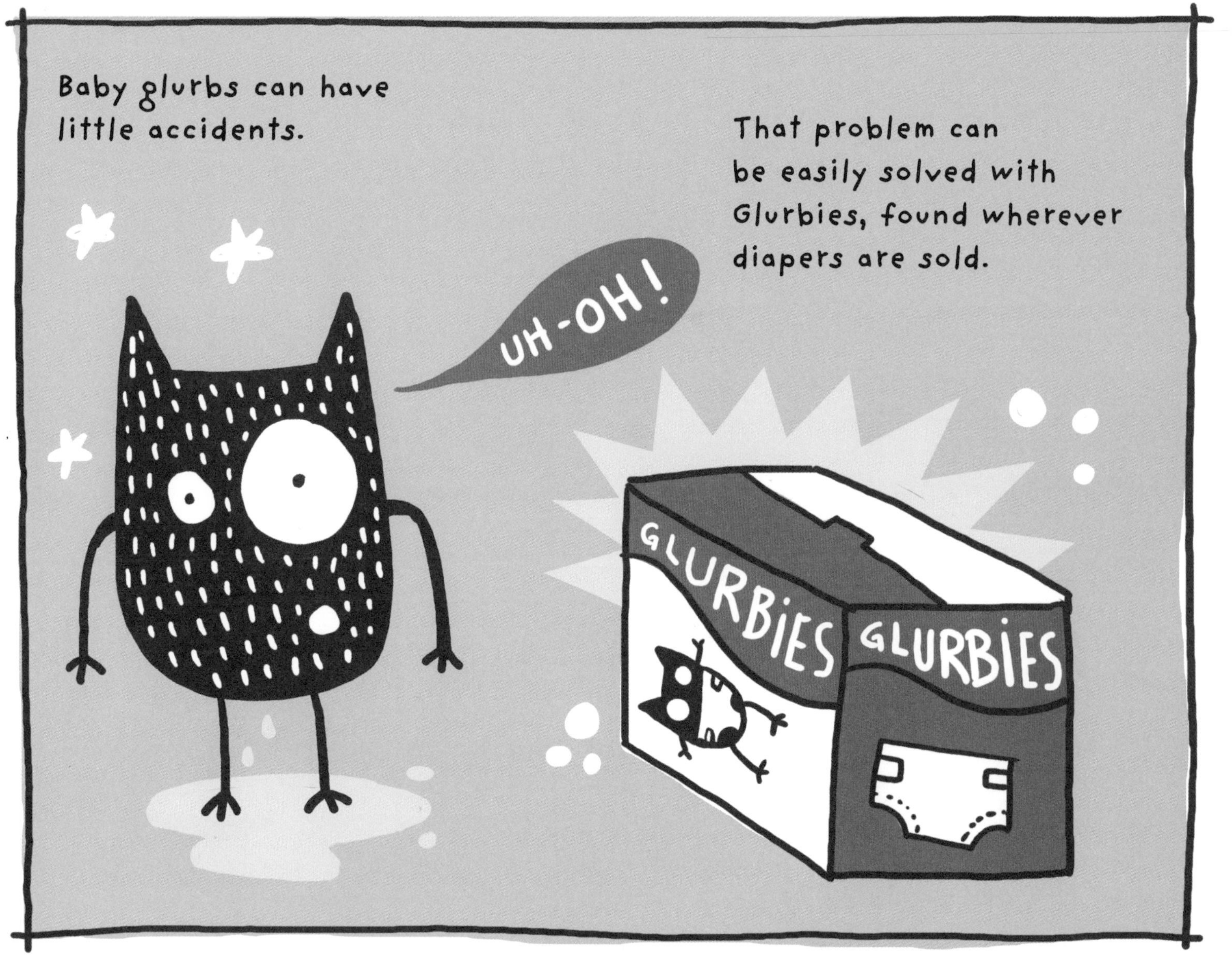
UH-OH!
GLURBIES
GLURBIES

Keep your glurb CLEAN

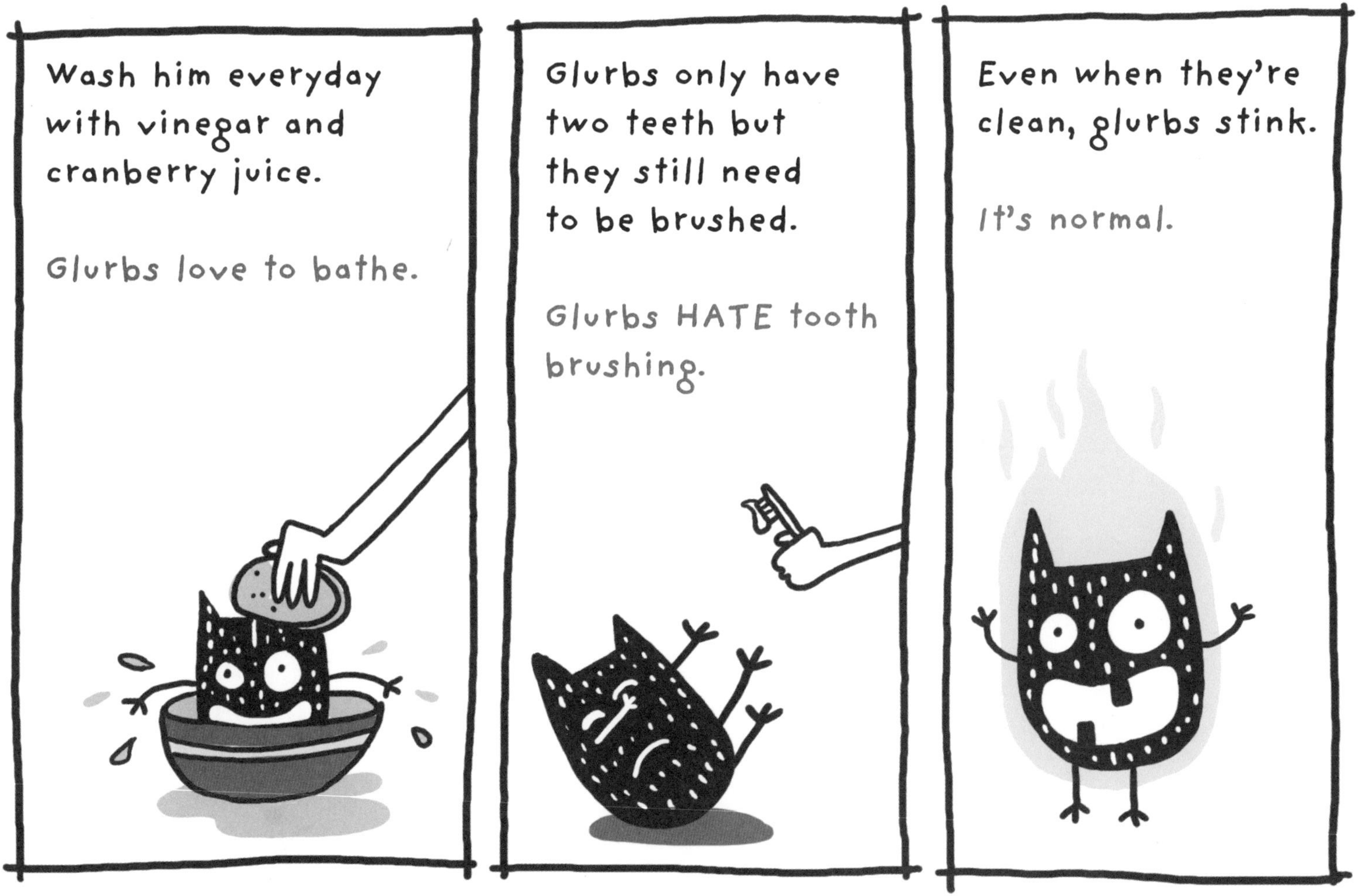

Wash him everyday with vinegar and cranberry juice.
Glurbs love to bathe.
Glurbs only have two teeth but they still need to be brushed.
Glurbs HATE tooth brushing.
Even when they're clean, glurbs stink.
It's normal.

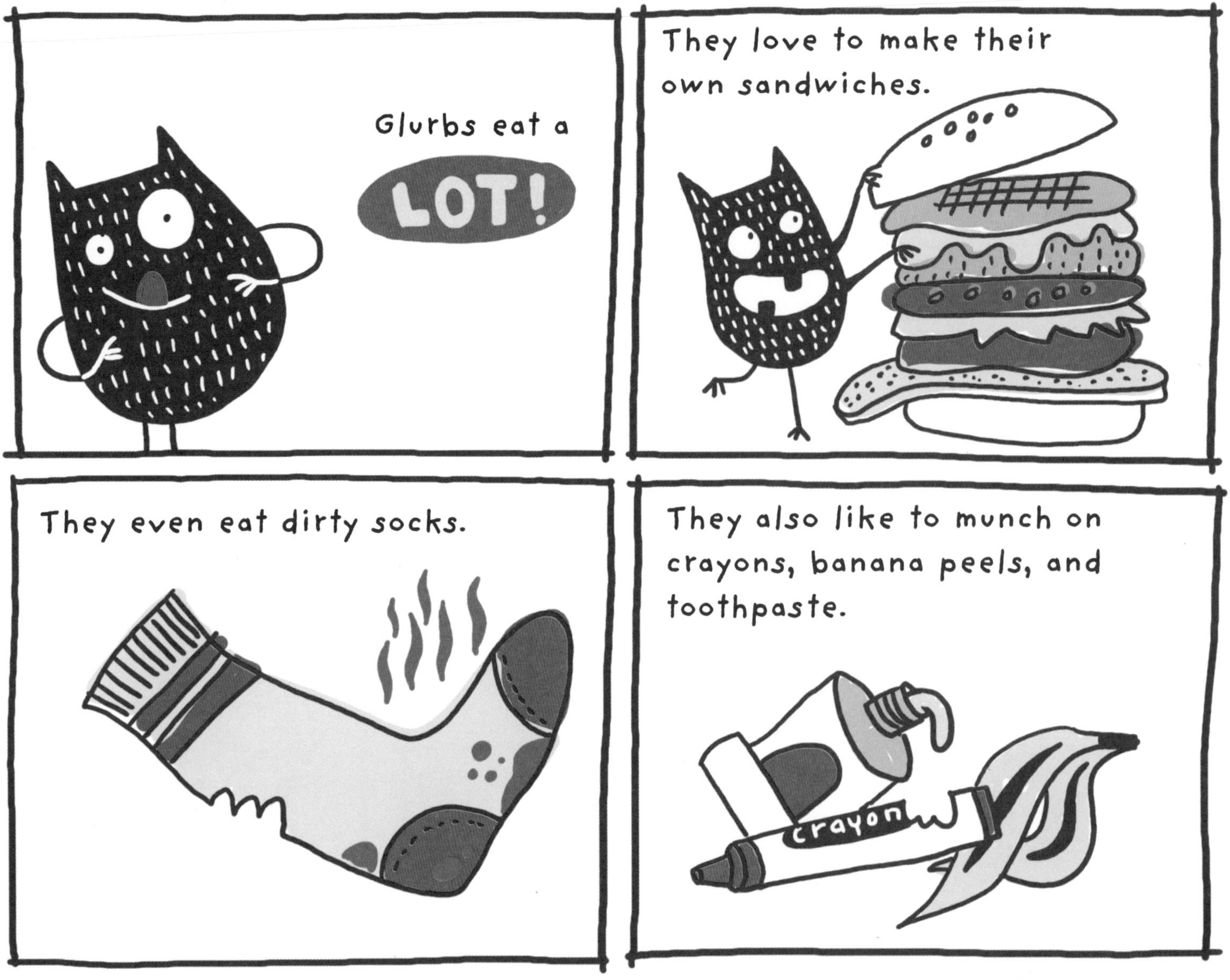
Glurbs eat a
LOT!
They love to make their own sandwiches.
They even eat dirty socks.
They also like to munch on crayons, banana peels, and toothpaste.
crayon

A glurb eats 10 times its own weight every day. Make sure to have a fridge full of its favorite foods.

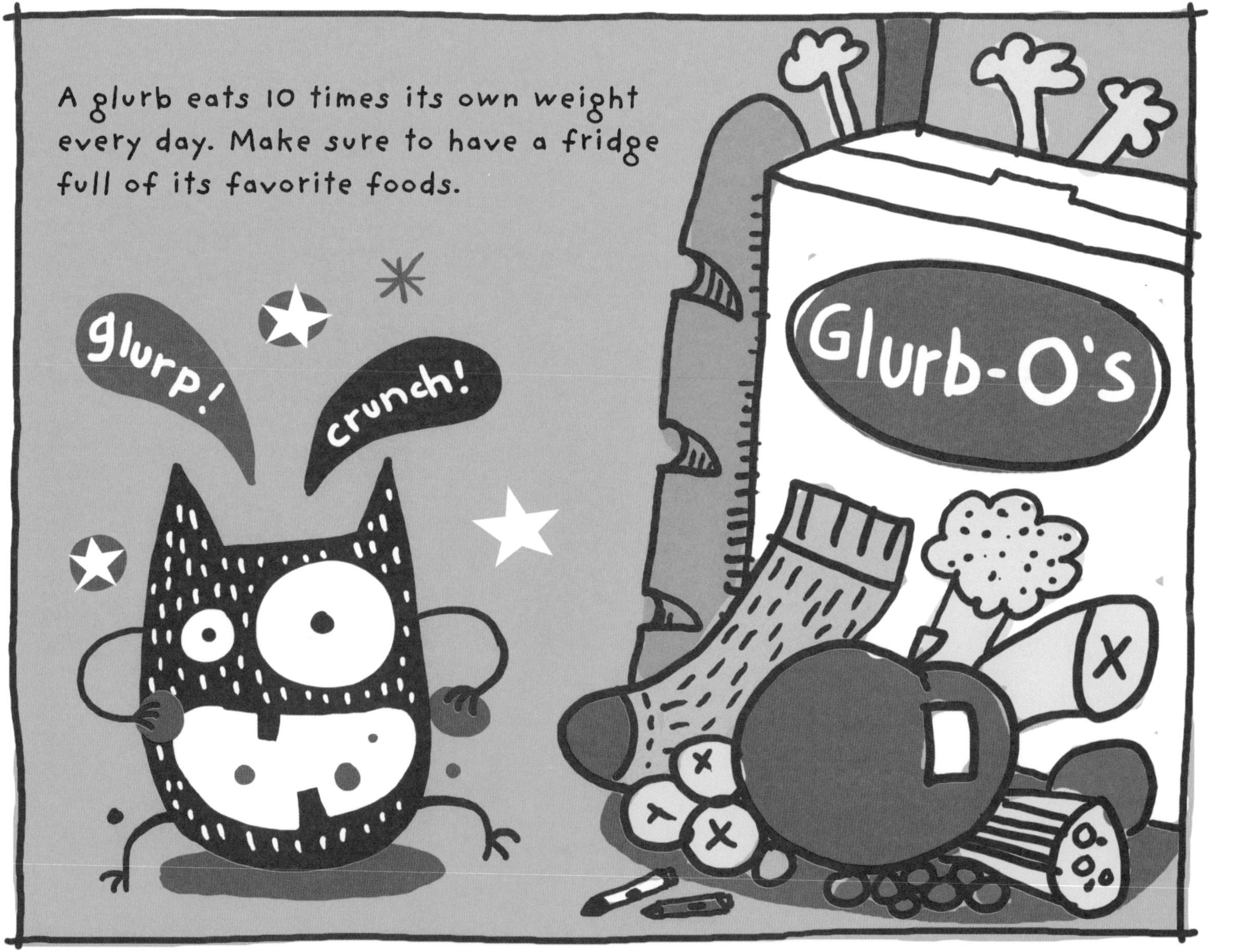
glurp!
crunch!
Glurb-O's

ACTIVITIES TO KEEP YOUR GLURB HAPPY

1 GOO

Glurbs love everything gooey: wet play-dough, mashed bananas, melting jell-o.

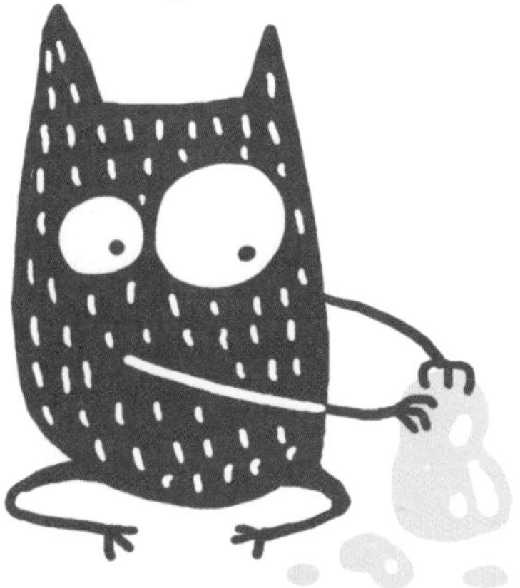

2 MUSIC

They LOVE music, especially jazz. They're also good dancers.

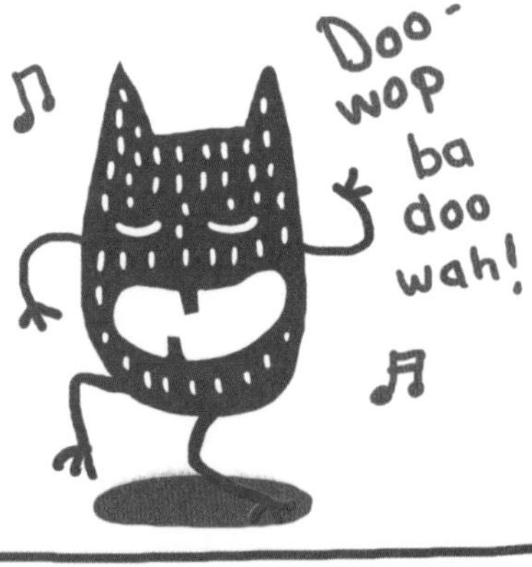
Doo-wop ba doo wah!

3 SLUG-RAISING

Glurbs like to play with slugs and slugs like to play with glurbs.

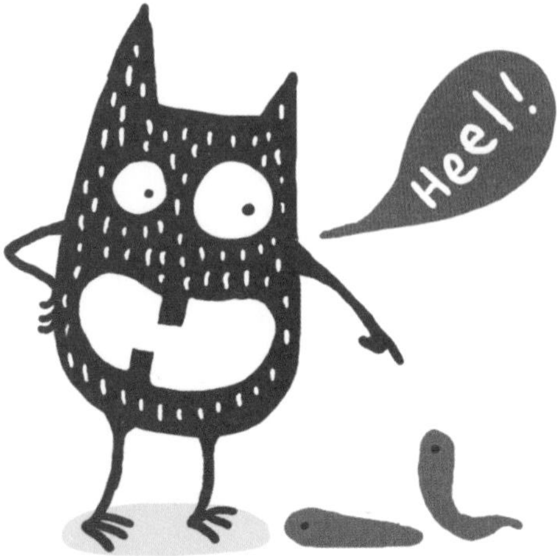
Heel!

If you give your glurb
a paper airplane,
he'll have lots of fun flying
around the house.

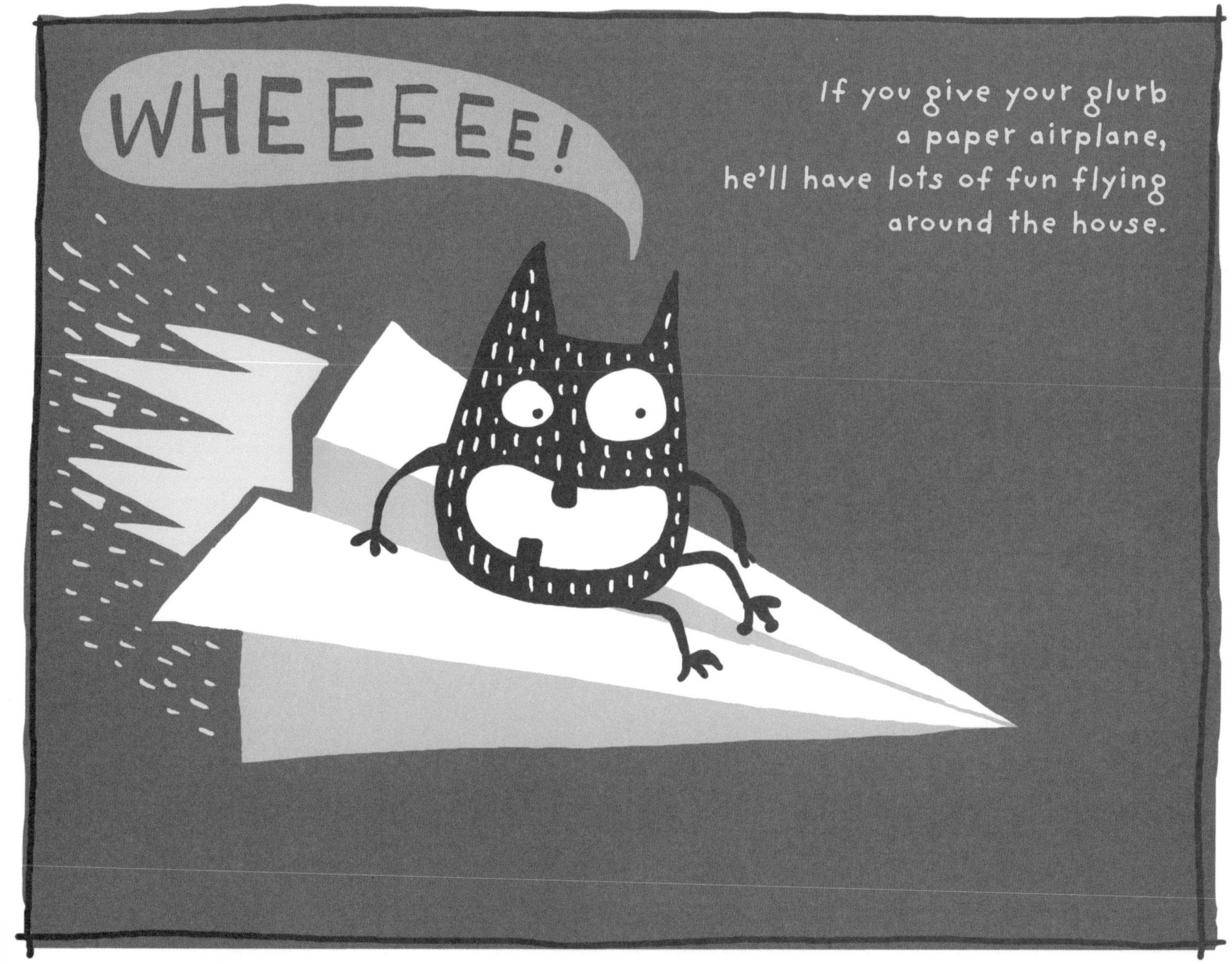
WHEEEEE!

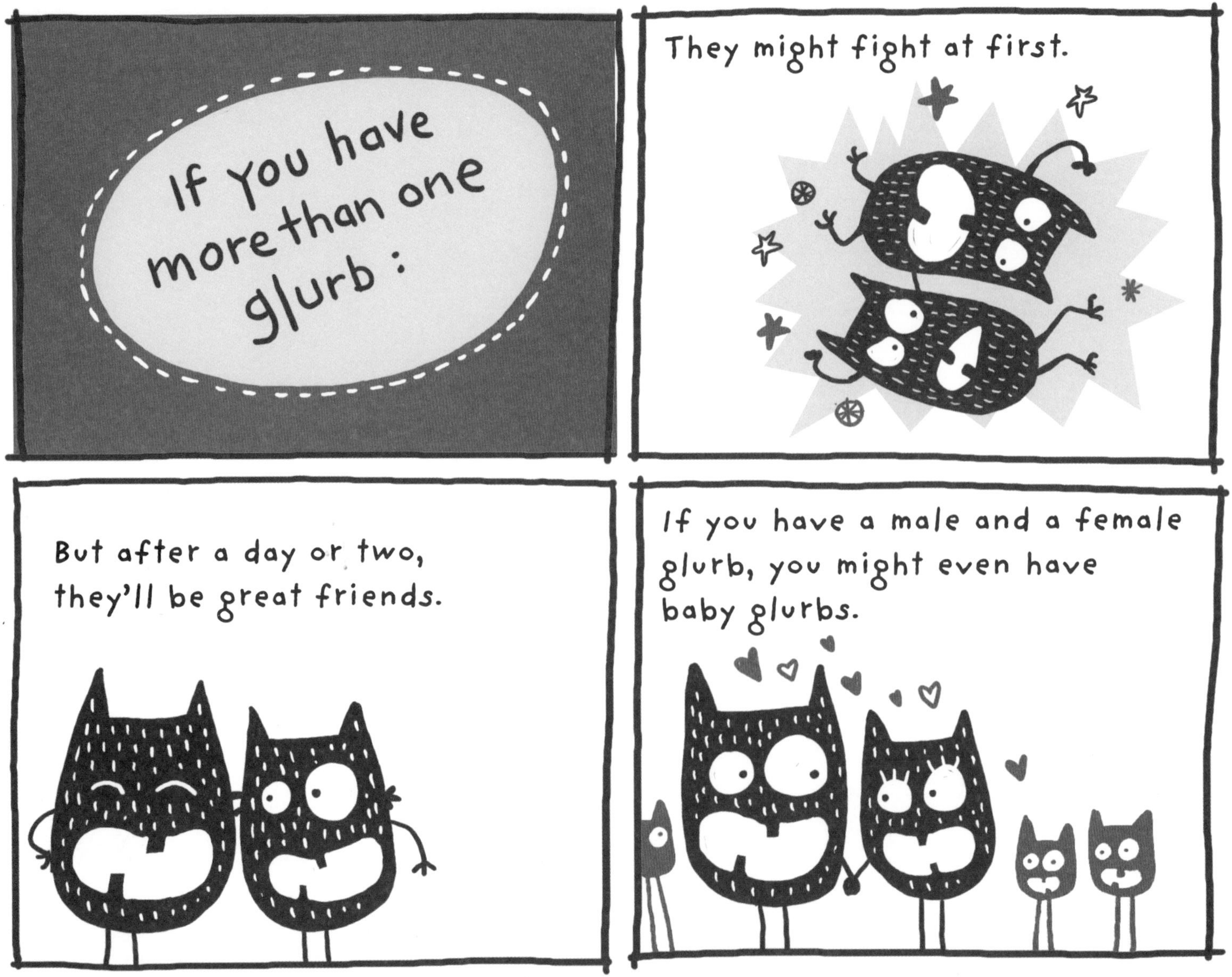
If you have more than one glurb:
They might fight at first.
But after a day or two, they'll be great friends.
If you have a male and a female glurb, you might even have baby glurbs.

Glurbs love to tell each other jokes—
but no one else understands what's funny.

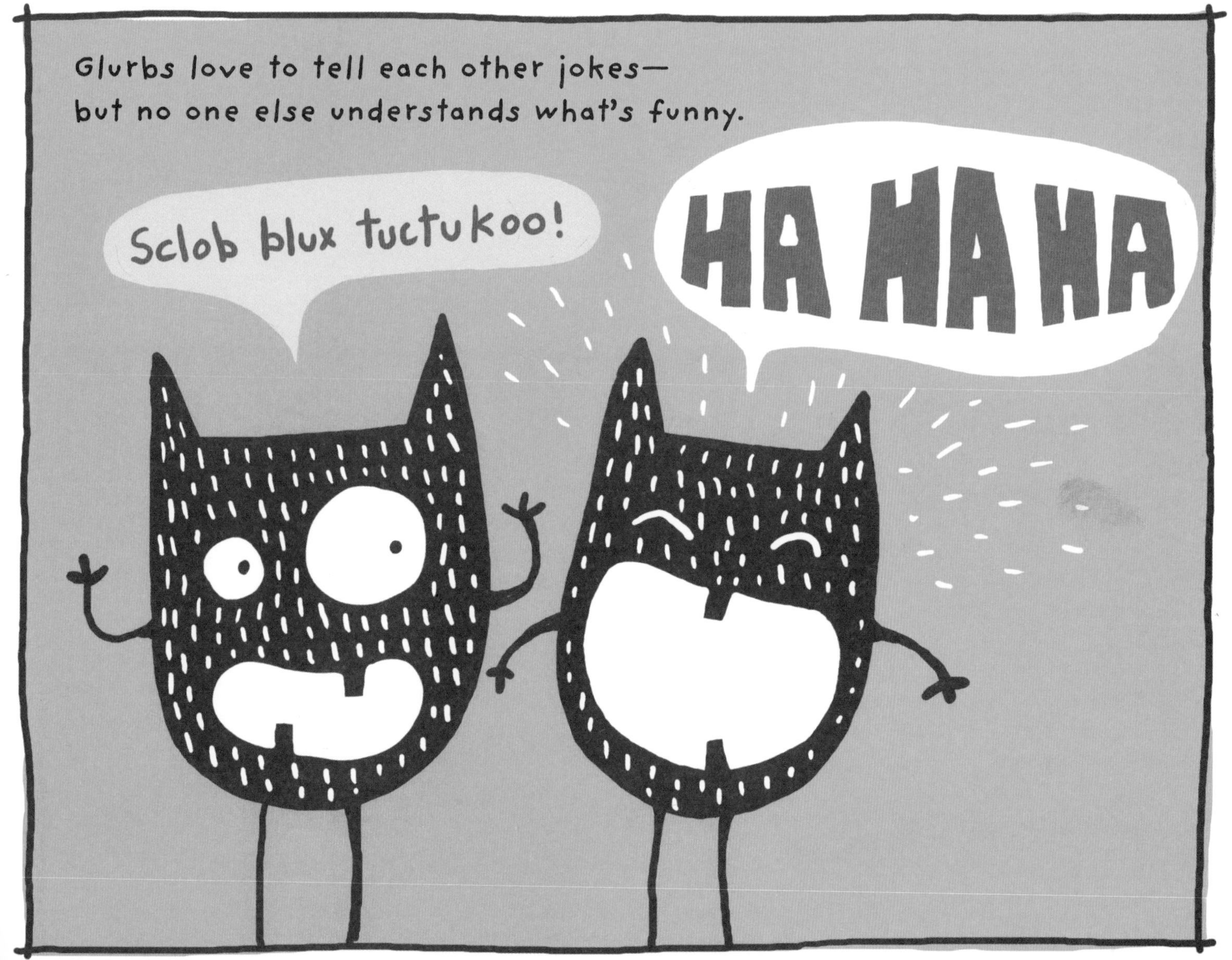
Sclob blux tuctukoo!
HA HA HA

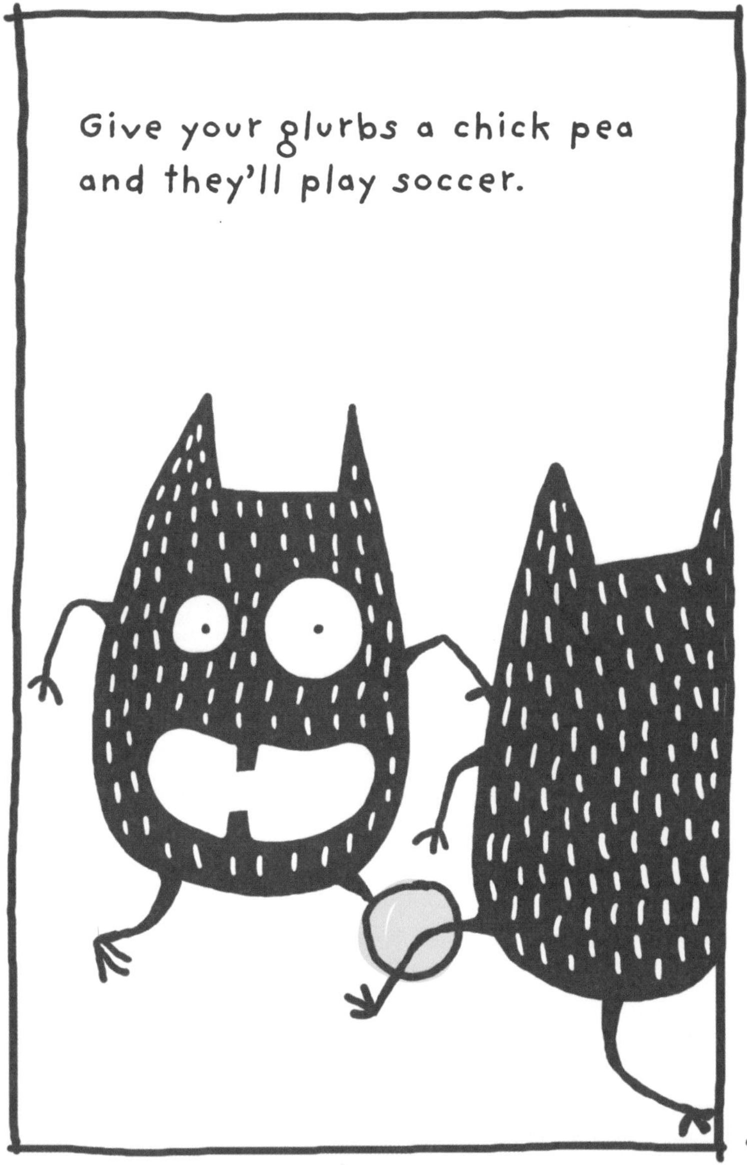
Give your glurbs a chick pea
and they'll play soccer.

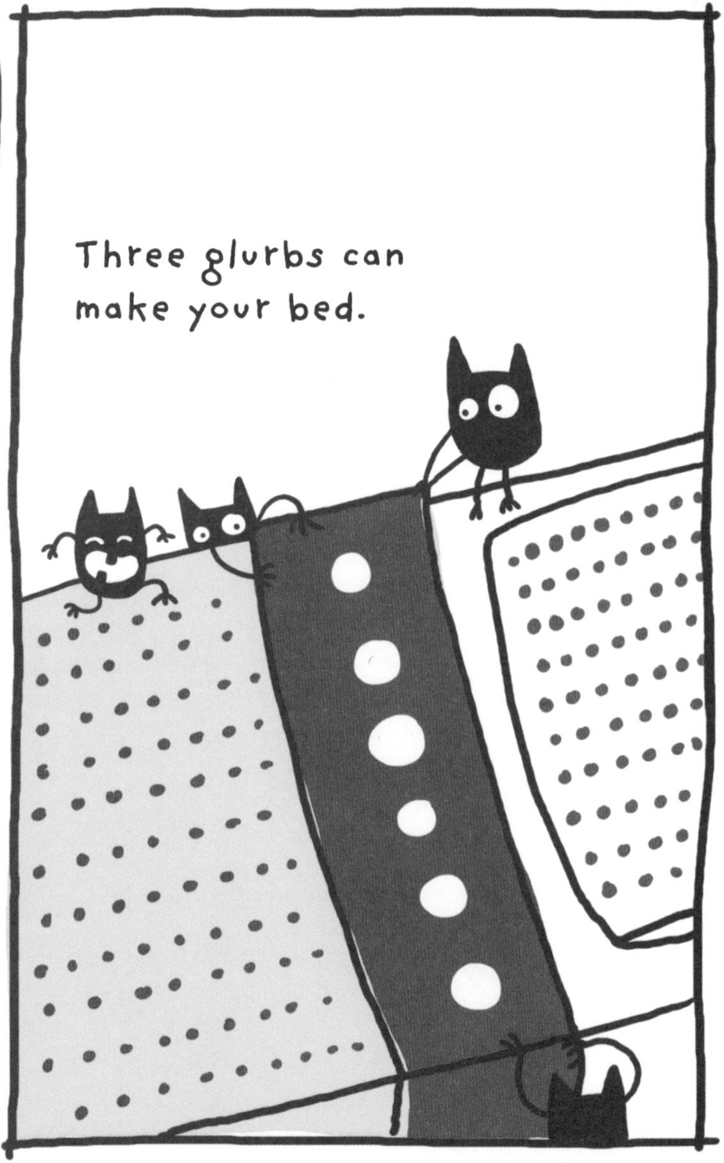
Three glurbs can
make your bed.

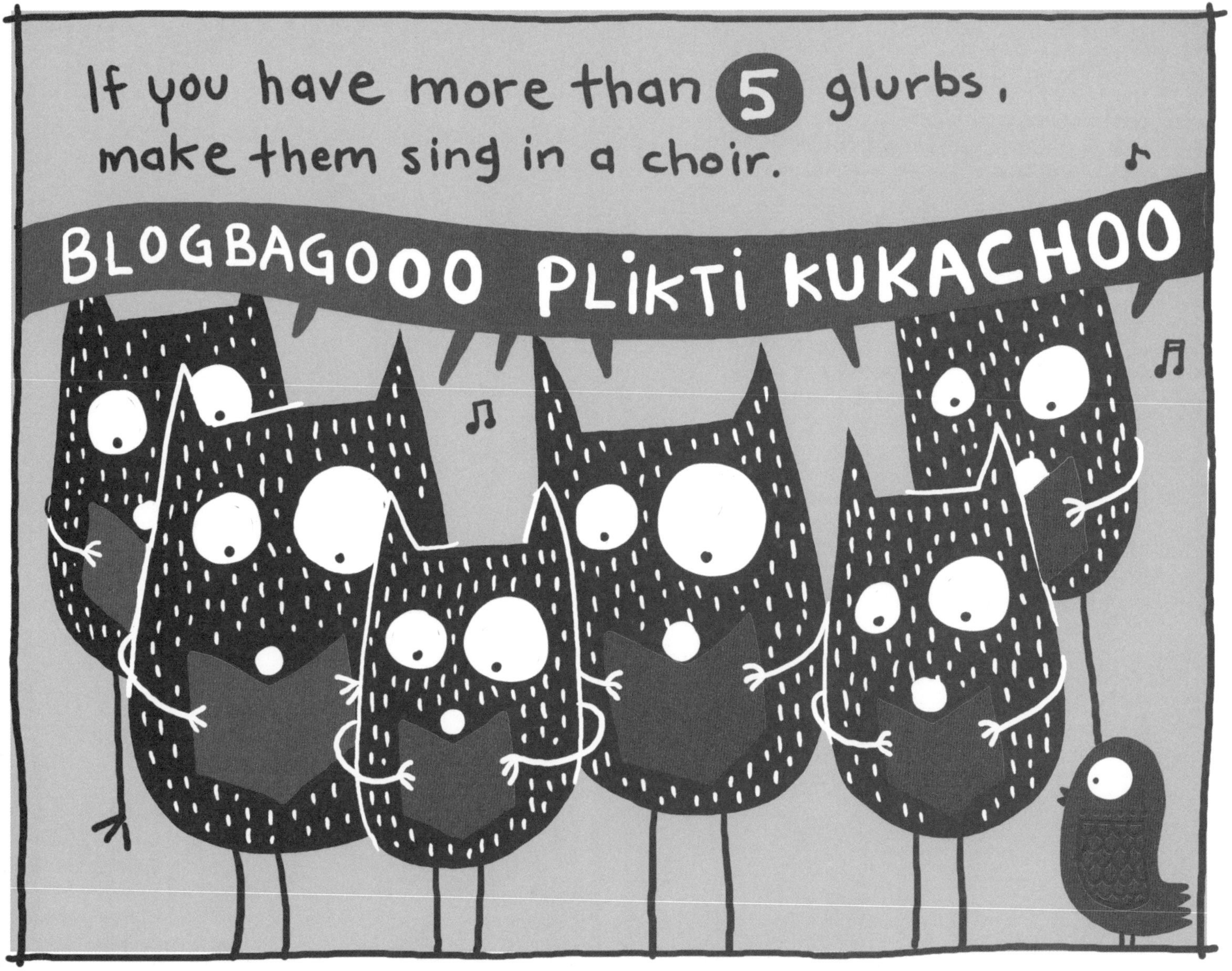
If you have more than 5 glurbs, make them sing in a choir.
BLOGBAGOOO PLIKTI KUKACHOO

Of course, if you have many glurbs, you'll need:

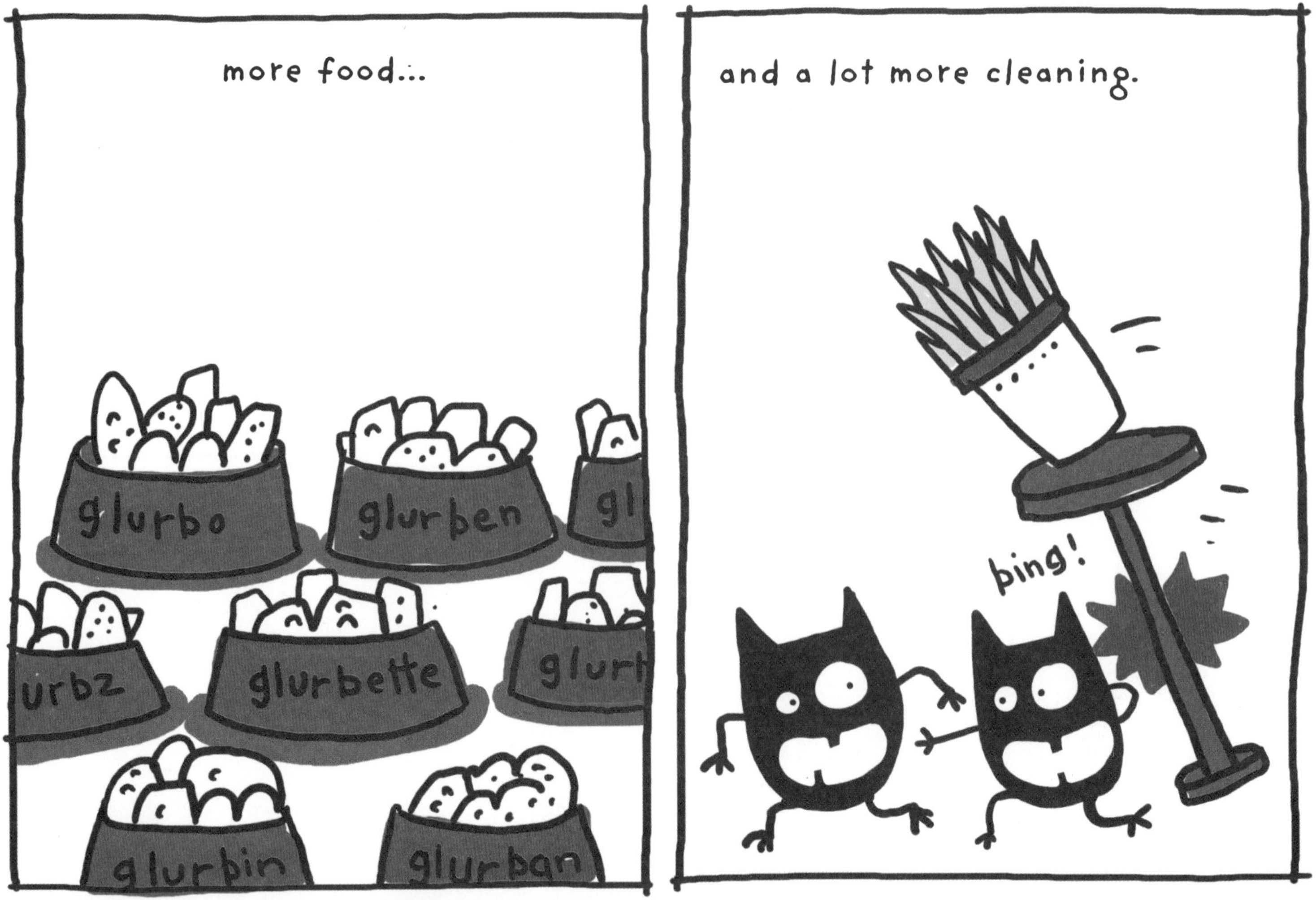
more food...
glurbo
glurben
gl
urbz
glurbette
glurt
glurbin
glurban
and a lot more cleaning.
bing!

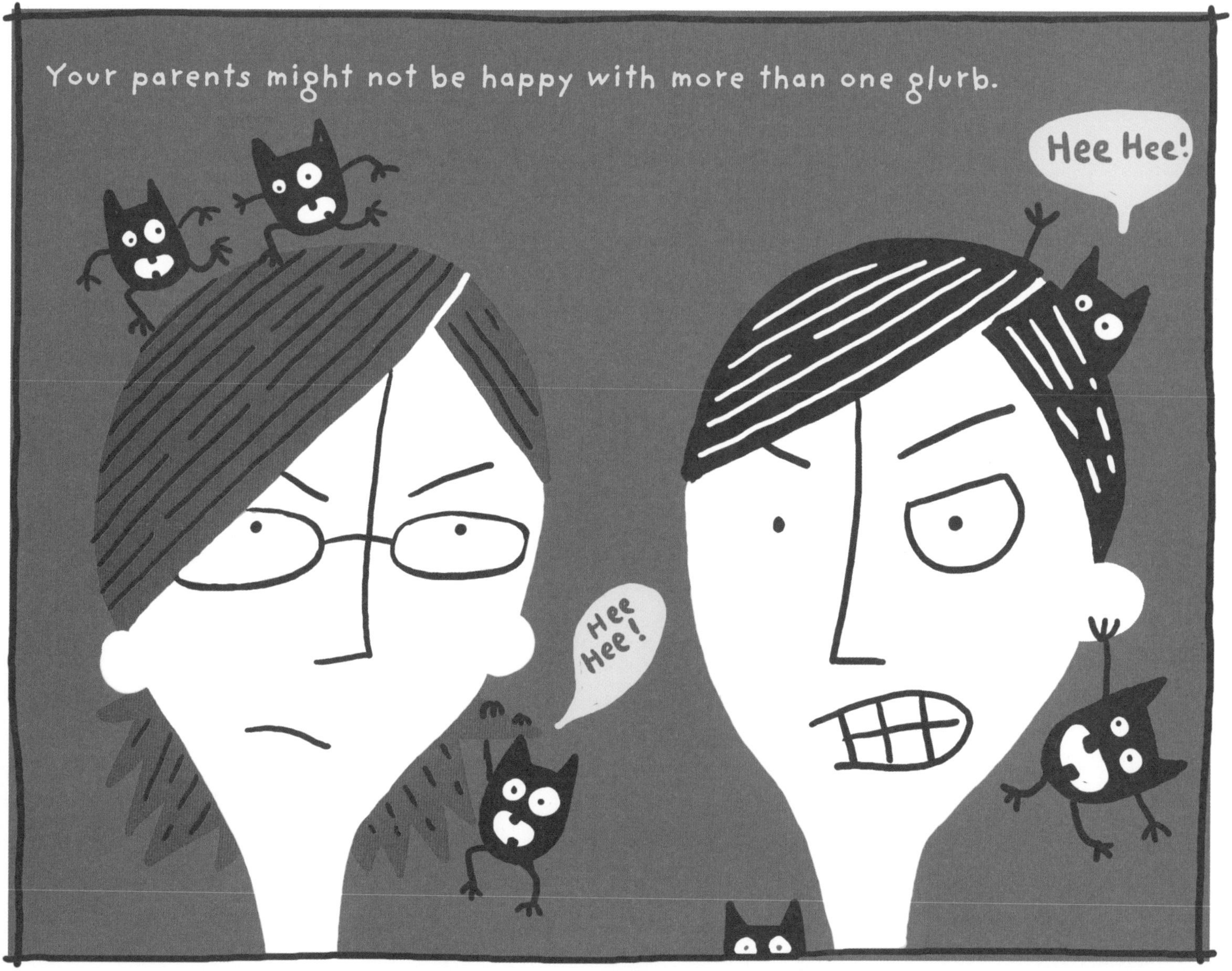
Your parents might not be happy with more than one glurb.
Hee Hee!
Hee Hee!

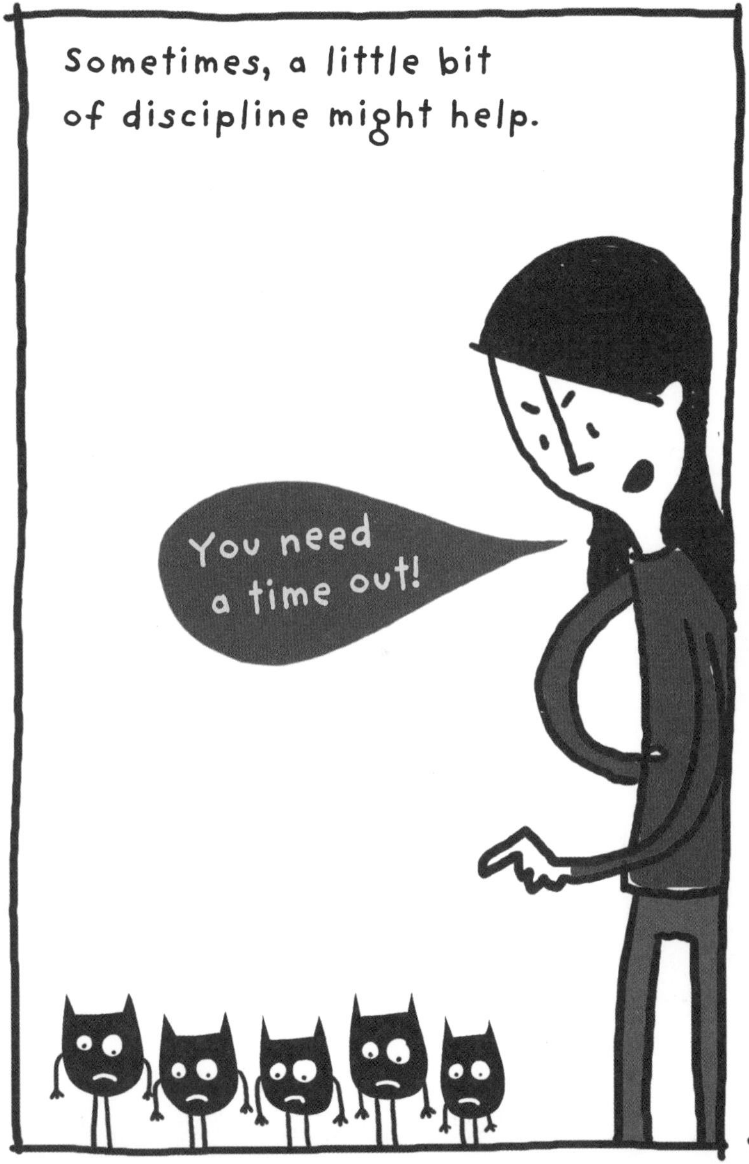
Sometimes, a little bit of discipline might help.
You need a time out!

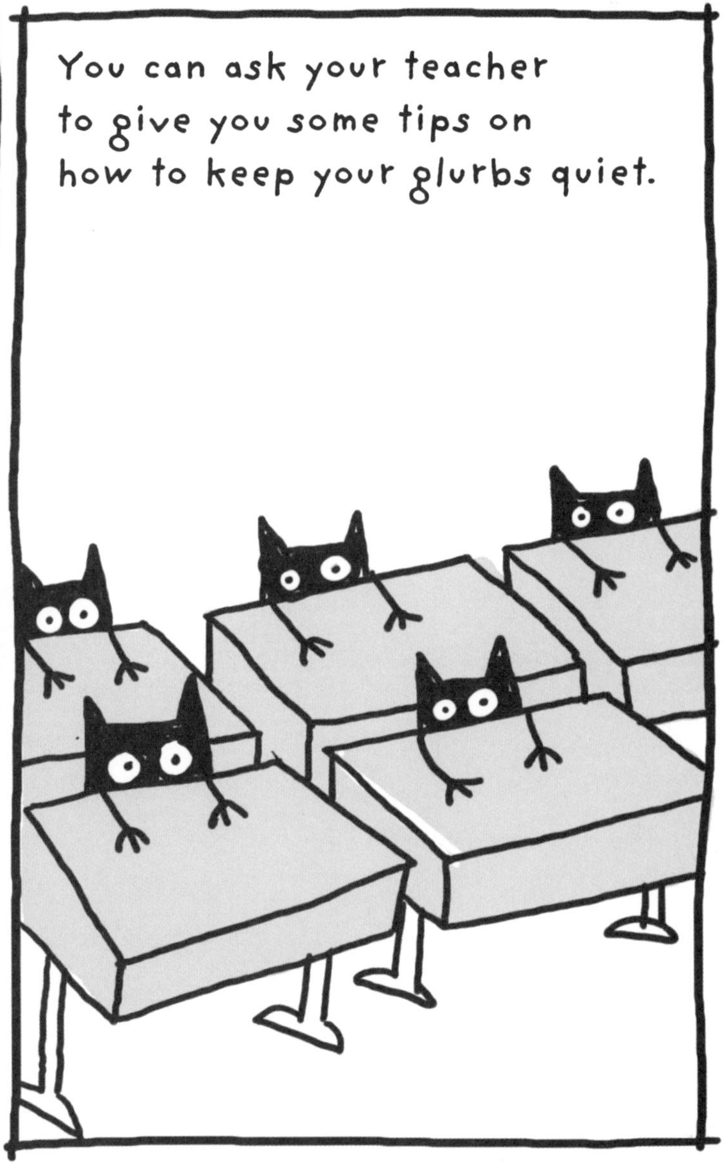
You can ask your teacher to give you some tips on how to keep your glurbs quiet.

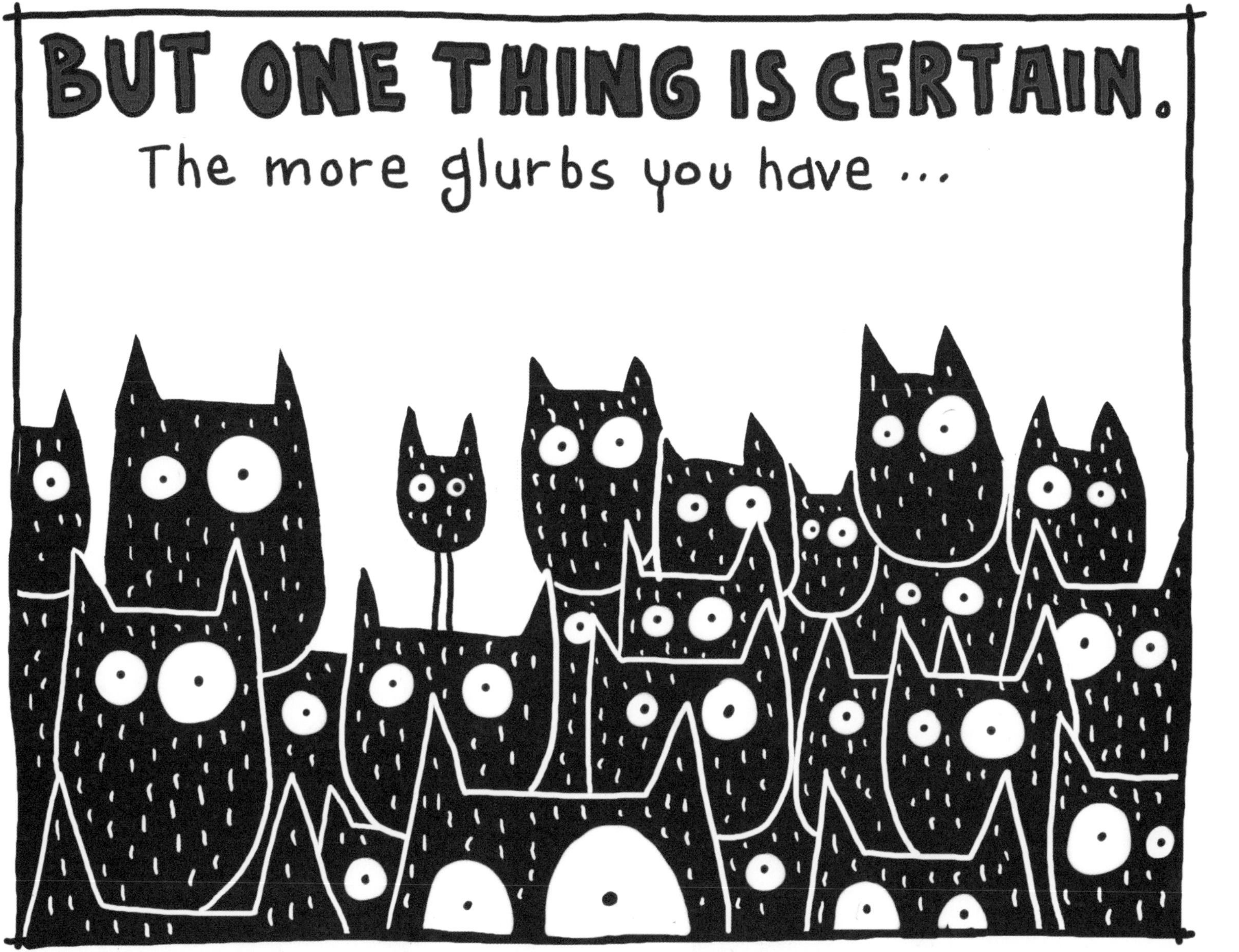
BUT ONE THING IS CERTAIN.
The more glurbs you have ...

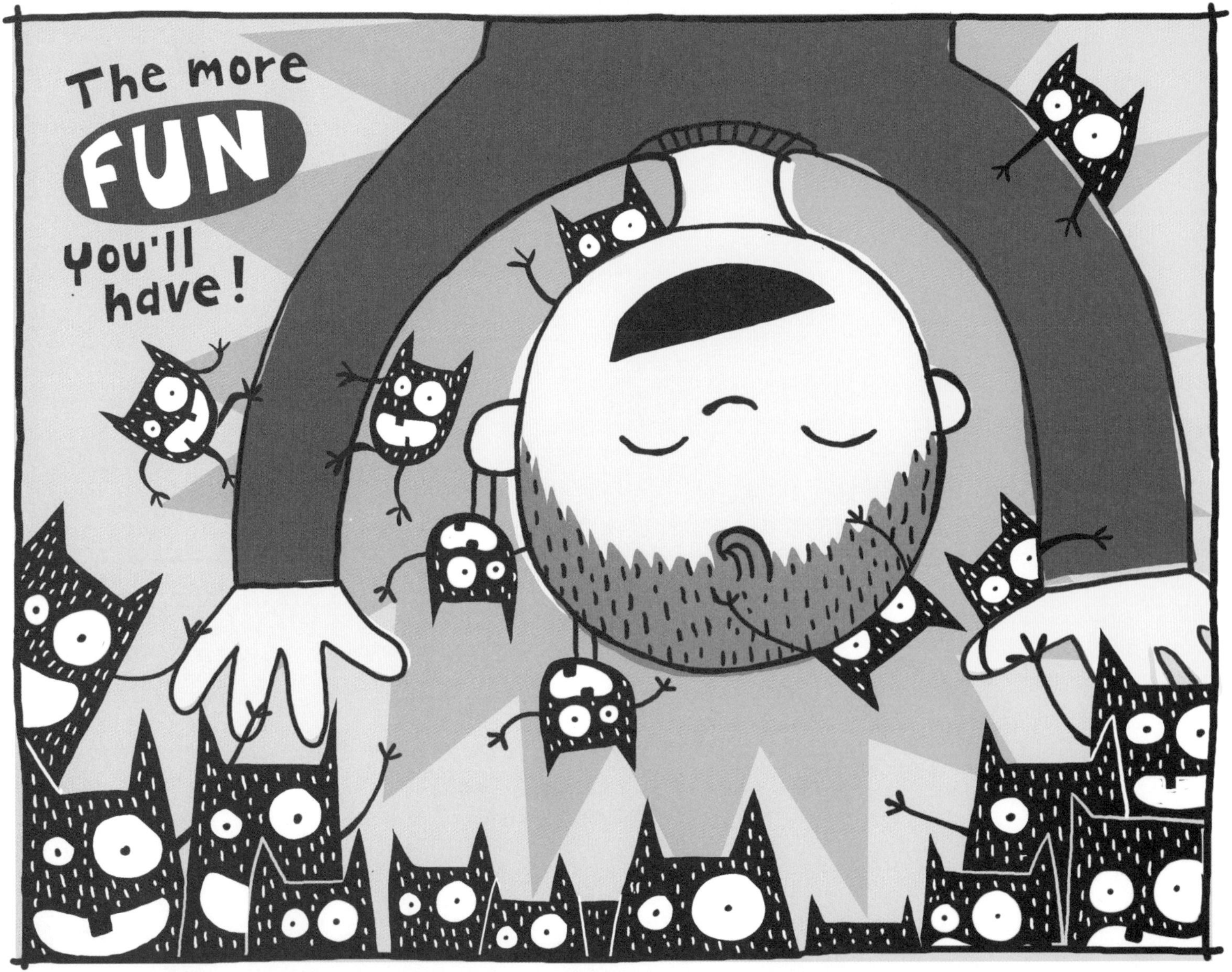
The more FUN you'll have!